WEB OF DESIRE #1

SPARK

Book #1 of the WEB OF DESIRE trilogy

ALEATHA ROMIG
New York Times, Wall Street Journal, and USA Today
bestselling author of the Consequences, Infidelity, Web of Sin,
and Tangled Web series

COPYRIGHT AND LICENSE INFORMATION

SPARK

Book #1 of the WEB OF DESIRE trilogy
Copyright @ 2020 Romig Works, LLC
Published by Romig Works, LLC
2020 Edition
ISBN: 978-1-947189-45-4
Cover art: Kellie Dennis at Book Cover by Design
(www.bookcoverbydesign.co.uk)
Editing: Lisa Aurello
Formatting: Romig Works, LLC

2020 Edition License

SYNOPSIS

SPARK – book #1 WEB OF DESIRE

"From a little spark may burst a flame." ~ **Dante Alighieri**

A simple ember to dried kindling can ignite a raging fire.

I've made my mark and proven my loyalty to a man, a city, and a way of life. That loyalty has provided me with all the spoils of success. For the longest time, that hasn't included a woman at my side.

There is only one beauty that can bring my untapped desire to life.

I shouldn't have opened the door. Cracking open the stone and striking the flint is my doing. What follows is hers.

With something so intense, will this spark lead to a blazing inferno? Will we make it out of the ashes before everything I hold dear is ravaged?

From New York Times bestselling author Aleatha Romig comes a brand-new dark romance, *Spark*, set in the same dangerous world as *Secrets and Twisted*. You do not need to read the *Web of Sin* or *Tangled Web* trilogy to get caught up in this new and intriguing saga, *Web of Desire*.

SPARK is book one of the *WEB OF DESIRE* trilogy that continues in *FLAME* and concludes in *ASHES*.

Have you been Aleatha'd?

PROLOGUE

Maddie
Twenty years ago

*B*e invisible.

It was my motto, my mantra, and my life.

With my chin down, eyes up, and hands tucked into the pocket of the oversized sweatshirt, I leaned against the brick wall, watching the world around me. It was hard not to stick out in Chicago's heat with the clothes I wore. Other people were wearing season-appropriate clothes such as shorts and tank tops.

My sweatshirt covered a t-shirt—the two shirts I owned. It would be nice to take off the sweatshirt, but I didn't have anywhere to store my belongings. The worn hiking boots upon my feet also didn't work for the season, but my assortment of sandals was currently nonexistent. The same was true of my long jeans. I could cut them, but that wouldn't do me any good when winter came.

Looking upward, I peered at the green leaves hanging from the giant maples. Soon their time would end. They'd change their colors and lose their hold. That was my measurement of time, seasons and hours of light. The days were longer and the nights warmer in the summer. Soon they'd begin to shorten and cool. This would be my second winter living on the street, and the first one had taught me well.

I tried to make myself smaller as the sidewalk around me bustled with people of all ages hurrying past. Chubby kids held tightly to their mothers' hands, complaining about life's unfairness. Men in uniforms went about their work. They weren't police or military but deliverymen, plumbers, and carpenters wearing shirts sporting their names. Store owners swept the street outside their businesses as if they could clean away the filth.

It was another day in paradise and I was part of the crowd.

Not the crowd who lived in the rundown apartments or even those who had the luxury of avoiding this area of the city. I was part of the faceless society that lingered in the shadows.

As the hot, humid late summer air refused to move, it was clear that Chicago had forgotten its nickname. For a moment, I pushed the hood of my sweatshirt off my head and stretched my neck to the blue sky, hoping for some relief.

Catcalls and whistles came from two tall boys passing by, reminding me to do what I did, to cover my growing hair and slither back to where I was out of harm's way, where I wouldn't be seen. It wasn't only safety I sought—it was also invisibility.

Safety was an elusive bitch but also a great teacher.

She wrapped you in warm blankets and tucked you into a soft bed.

She told you stories of princesses, princes, and knights on white horses.

She filled your mind with dreams and your belly with food.

She held you tight and chased away the monsters from under your bed and then, when you were content, she left you alone, cold, crying, and abandoned.

She'd taught me that nothing lasted.

Stepping back against the building, I kept my focus on the bins of fresh produce outside the corner store across the street. There were apples, bananas, and tomatoes. The truck had delivered them around sunrise, just as happened every day.

It was the best part of this time of year, fresh, juicy fruit, straight from some farm. That was the way I pictured it in my head, like something out of a child's picture book, a farm with green hills and an orchard with trees bursting with apples. In the morning, the sunlight would break through the morning mist, exposing a vibrant blue sky.

My stomach rumbled.

I'd been watching the store for over an hour. The owner was a crotchety old man who spoke briskly to his patrons while shunning the likes of me. I supposed he and his wife worked hard. The two of them were there every day except Sundays. On that day, the store was closed with grates covering the windows. The couple's routine was always the same. One worked inside while the other kept a watchful eye on the sidewalk. This time of year, he would spend his day with a broom in hand. In the winter, it would be a shovel.

There were other options to fill my empty stomach, soup kitchens and the like. I hated their lines, their questions, and their feigned attempts to help. As a multiple-time foster-system failure, I'd wasted enough time listening to their sugary tones that did nothing more than coat their pious judgment with sweetness.

Being left without a family and a home didn't make me less than them. I didn't want their pity or their handouts. Each encounter strengthened my resolve: one day I would not only survive, but I'd overcome.

Today wasn't that day.

Nevertheless, I wasn't looking for handouts; I was looking at opportunity in the form of produce in the bins. If an apple would drop to the concrete, the owner would throw it away.

Why not reallocate it instead?

My gaze kept focused on the polished red fruit. I didn't know why, but there was something about the apples I couldn't shake.

As if divined by God, the sun's rays shone down, reflecting upon their shiny ruby skins and calling to me, even from the other side of the street.

An hour passed and then another.

After a while the hungry stomach succumbs to its state, forgetting to grumble and growl.

The sun was high when a woman with a small child in tow asked something of the owner. Nodding, he'd led the paying customers inside. It was the break I'd been waiting for, my chance to procure my own breakfast-slash-lunch.

My gaze darted from side to side as I hurried across the street, weaving in and out of parked cars and delivery trucks.

One apple would feed me.

One would fit into the pocket of my sweatshirt without notice.

One could easily disappear.

My steps stilled near the bin. Hunger roared back to life, twisting my stomach. Saliva formed as I imagined my teeth piercing the firm red outer skin as the apple's juice coated my tongue.

One.

A second one.

I reached for one more.

"Hey, you thief!"

As the third apple fell to the concrete below, my feet began to move.

I weaved in and out of people, turning down one alley and then another. Perspiration dripped beneath the heavy sweatshirt as I continued to run.

The heavy beat of footsteps sounded farther and farther behind. Though I was breathing heavily, my youth and agility gave me the speed and distance. The shout and pursuit had not come from the store owner or his wife but from a policeman. I'd been too focused on my bounty to realize he was near. A beat cop, he was at the bottom of the police totem pole. Thankfully his beer belly reduced his athletic ability.

Turning the corner, I nearly collided with another policeman, a younger officer, speaking into his shoulder. The chase was on again.

This one was more difficult to outrun; however, hunger was a strong motivator.

It wasn't only the loss of the apples that would occur if I was caught.

Incarceration would follow, and worst yet, reentry into the foster care system.

If I listened to the counselors, they'd say it also meant a roof over my head and three meals a day. I supposed that depended upon the foster parents. Nevertheless, in my experience, the negatives outweighed the positives.

With my pulse pounding, I ran down a different alley. The stench of trash overflowing the dumpsters was my friend, hopefully warding off my pursuer. Ducking behind a large metal container, I leaned forward, catching my breath.

"Hey," I tried to scream as a hand came over my mouth and my arm was tugged backward. My mind raced with possibilities. Whoever had me wasn't a policeman, yet no matter how I struggled, I couldn't break his hold. My hood slipped from my head.

"Shh." The warning came with a warm breath to my ear.

Though my boots tried to stay steadfast, I was pulled backward until we slipped through an opening in the brick wall, leading to a dark space.

"Don't talk," the boy's voice whispered. "Nod if you'll stay quiet."

My head bobbed as the sound of footsteps echoed from beyond the dumpster, the one blocking the opening. Slowly my captor's hand released me and I turned to see the space around me. My eyes adjusted to the lack of light as the room came into view. The space wasn't large, although the ceiling was high enough for us to stand. I continued to take it in, knowing that with an old sleeping bag upon stacks of old newspapers along the far wall, this was obviously where this person slept.

With trepidation, my gaze met my assailant's.

The fear that had been building within me was replaced by something I hadn't felt since my life imploded. There was something in this tall boy's eyes that gave me the unfamiliar sense of safety.

"What do you want?" I asked, painfully aware that he was male and I was female.

"I was just trying to help you," he said with a grin. "It was a lame move for the pig to call for backup. Hell, it's just a couple apples. Or did you steal something more valuable?"

I'd almost forgotten the apples. My fists came to my hips. "Right, I have the Hope Diamond concealed under my shirt."

"Damn, I was hoping for food."

"Is that why you pulled me in here, to take my apples?" I asked.

Shaking his head, he gestured toward the opening. "I mean, you can go if you want. Good luck."

"Wait." I turned completely around in the small space. When our gazes again met, I noticed his dirty cheeks and how they made his blue eyes and blond hair more prominent. "Tell me why you pulled me in here."

He shrugged his broad yet skinny shoulder. "I've seen you around, and well, like I said, the cop was lame. I wanted to help you."

"First, I don't need your help or anyone else's."

Without a word he again gestured toward the door.

This makeshift room wasn't the Hilton or even a Motel 6,

but it wasn't bad once I became accustomed to the stench from the dumpster "If I stay, what will you do? What do you want?"

Stepping back to the dirty sleeping bag, the boy sat, crossed his legs, and looked up at me. It was a simple move that without words told me he wasn't a threat, at least not right now.

He tilted his head. "I didn't save you for a reward. But now that you're here." He nodded toward my sweatshirt. "I'd really like one of those apples."

A smile came to my face as I looked down at how the apples were obviously within the front pocket. Reaching into the pocket, I pulled out one with each hand. They didn't vary a lot, but one was bigger. I lifted the larger one and handed it his direction. "Thank you for saving me."

He reached for the apple and grinned a friendly smile. "Thanks for the food."

I nodded toward his make-do bed. "Do you mind if I have a seat too?"

"Not at all." He scooted to one side.

A hum escaped my lips as I bit into the apple. It was as firm and juicy as I'd predicted. When I turned, he was still looking at me. Wiping my hand on my jeans, I lifted it to the boy. "Hi, I'm Maddie."

He took it and we shook. "I'm Patrick, welcome to my place."

Again I stared at the space. "I like what you've done with it."

Pink came to his cheeks as he took another bite. "It's not much, but it's mostly dry. And the dumpster out there keeps other people away. Not the mice and rats, but that's what that is for." He pointed.

In the corner was a piece of dirty plywood.

"You've got everything you need."

"How about a friend?" he asked.

There's no way to describe the feeling of security, and I knew it wouldn't last, but with this boy, I felt safe, and for the first time in two years, in his space, I felt at home.

PATRICK

Present day

A con.
A fake.

A phony.

A thief.

I could spot one from across the room. Forget that. I could spot one from thousands of miles away with nothing more than a picture or post on social media. That ability had kept me alive from a very young age. Life was a great teacher, and I'd learned my lessons well.

With time and tenacity, I had overcome what many couldn't or didn't. Between the GI bill and some help from a friend, I had more than life's lessons. I also had an education. The degrees in business and finance supplemented the accumulation of my experiences. Together it allowed me to excel at many things. My interests and abilities were vast; however, it was watching, analyzing, and understanding people that I kept honed. That simple tool of observation kept me at the top of my game.

In my life, my world, the consequence of losing was death.

Currently, my sights were set on an exquisitely beautiful woman. There were countless reasons why she'd garner my attention or that of any red-blooded male. Of course, those reasons were in my mind. Yet my attraction was focused on more than her appearance.

Even from this distance I knew she wasn't exactly what she appeared to be.

While the alarm bells were ringing, I couldn't look away.

Working as I did with my associates and those who worked under me wouldn't be possible if I wasn't able to read expressions and anticipate reactions. If a person was being genuine, each reaction varied by some degree. It didn't matter if the person was male or female, rich or poor, educated or not, or even intelligent or not.

No, education didn't equate to intelligence. The streets were full of people with intelligence—street smarts—who may not have seen a classroom since a very young age.

Appearance meant little. Beauty was most often simply a veneer. Some of the darkest, coldest hearts I'd encountered were covered by the prettiest of packages.

I supposed I could qualify in that regard.

While I'd been a skinny, starving kid, that was in my past.

Though taking me on a tortuous long road, fate had ultimately been kind.

A desperate decision landed me in the right place with the right group of guys. Those guys were now men, and together, we ruled this city. Some referred to what we did as the underground or organized crime. In some respects, they were right.

We were incredibly organized.

And we dealt in many activities that some would consider crimes.

One could either ignore the existence of this world or flourish within its realm. For better or worse, I was a piece of Chicago's puzzle, part of the Sparrow outfit.

Sterling Sparrow's name was on the buildings, respected in high society, and whispered in the dark alleyways. Nevertheless, the saying was true: no man is an island. Success at the level of the Sparrow outfit wasn't accomplished alone. It took a trusted team.

It took men capable of looking death in the face, washing blood off our hands, and coming back for more, all while appearing refined. Maintaining our wolf-in-sheep's-clothing appearance was part of our success.

There were other names besides Sterling Sparrow that evoked the appropriate respect, names that had been with Sparrow since the fateful night he acquired what had been his father's and more recently, to the afternoon when the city became united under one name.

One of those names that garnered respect was mine.

Patrick Kelly.

The skinny kid I'd once been grew into a man capable of more than he ever imagined.

Over the years, I'd moved on from my less-than-humble beginnings. I tended to my body and mind, growing both, refining both, until they were perfected.

I'd learned that to be truly intimidating it took more than an outward appearance. I had that, being called scary more than once. What was more frightening was a person with a clean shave and trimmed hair in an expensive designer suit and Italian loafers who was capable of the unthinkable. It was the illusion of civility that gave men like me and those I worked with and called my friends the advantage.

People ran from the boogeyman.

I was the man they ran toward.

In some cases, it's worked out well.

In others it was a deadly mistake.

The handsomer the face, the easier it was to deceive.

No longer a fighter striving to live on the streets, today I was part of the elite, the royalty of Chicago. If Sparrow were a true monarch, I supposed Reid, Mason, and I would be considered dukes or lords, those men appointed at the king's whim to stand beside and behind him, to risk body and soul for his success, because in doing so, we also ensured our own.

The three of us had repeatedly proven ourselves worthy of our accession. Today the boy who once slept in gutters and beneath underpasses lived in a glass castle high in Chicago's skyline. Today along with a chosen few, I ruled the same streets where I once scrounged for food and shelter.

While Chicago was our kingdom, the reach of the Sparrow name stretched beyond the city limits. Our armies marched throughout the country and beyond. Sparrow wasn't alone in his level of success. Other cities and other families held power. Nevertheless, each day we worked to expand the Sparrow umbrella, to make nice when possible and topple if necessary.

One was either the arrow or the target.

The Sparrow outfit was the arrow.

My gaze zeroed in again upon the extraordinary beauty across the room—my target—for tonight's discovery. A ghost from the past, she brought my worlds colliding. My past and present were now both here.

Seeing her brought life where there had been death. Like a stray spark landing upon the dry underbrush of a forest, being in her presence lit my body on fire. My visceral reaction to her caught me unaware. My heart rate increased and my senses went on high alert.

It wasn't simply her beauty.

Daily, I was in the presence of beautiful, intelligent, and strong women. I respected their fortitude as much as the men's. Those women didn't cause my heart to race or breath to catch. The small hairs on my neck didn't stand to attention nor did my dick wake from its long hibernation.

As I took in her presence, I found myself both enthralled and somewhat dumbfounded that I was capable of such a visceral reaction. It wasn't as if I'd lived the life of a monk. I hadn't. Nonetheless, this was different. She was different.

I wasn't near enough to smell her perfume or feel her soft breath upon my skin. Yet from the way my body was reacting, I could be.

I had been.

That was before.

Time was a merciless bitch, stopping for no man or woman.

I never thought I'd see her again—that it was even possible —and yet with everything within me, I knew it was her when I first saw her. After all these years, she was back in my city as if she'd never left.

With her death never verified, over time, I had looked for her periodically. Each fruitless search was more confirmation of her demise.

That was until now, until tonight.

I entered this conference hall with the intention of overseeing the poker tournament at hand. It was a million-dollar tournament. That kind of money didn't change hands without Sparrow knowledge. Fate had brought me to Club Regal tonight, to this room.

The tournament's purse was big, and the bets being placed even now were impressive. Millions of dollars had come to our city, and I was here as a reminder that taxes were due. It wasn't that the players per se would hand me cash. The tournament itself would pass on a percentage to Sparrow. It was how it worked.

Imagine my surprise upon seeing her again after all this time.

With my errand at hand momentarily forgotten, I was staggered as years of memories flooded my mind along with a myriad of emotions.

Joy.

Anger.

Disbelief.

Uncertainty.

Shock.

Madeline was alive.

She'd never died.

As the disbelief faded, I had one conflicting thought.

Though I would always love her, now I hated her.

Parts of my mind had forgotten the woman I knew, put her aside. That was then. In the split second of seeing her, my body was reminded of all she'd been, that we'd been. Not many of us made it off the streets. Some died trying. Others died *not* trying —giving up or giving in.

Few went on to live in the lap of luxury.

While I wasn't certain of her living arrangements, by the appearance of our current surroundings and the stack of $1000 poker chips before her, she did not fear for her next meal. No one could place the monetary bets I'd watched her place—win or lose—without some financial stability. The high-stakes games that occurred on this floor of this private club couldn't be financed with good looks or credit.

After all these years, Madeline had returned, not as the pauper I'd known but as a member of the elite in her own right.

As I continued to take her in from afar, I couldn't help but marvel at her outward calm. She was a true showman when it came to this arena. In the last hour, I'd watched as she'd won thousands of dollars, make that tens of thousands, and lost equally as large pots. Her dark green eyes, the same ones that haunted my dreams over the years, remained steadfast.

However, Madeline had her tells.

I doubted the other players saw them.

The others were too busy calculating their own strategies of success, or perhaps, mesmerized by her beautiful packaging. It could be the way her raven black hair cascaded over her slender shoulders or her sensual neck straightened.

My mind tried to process the teenager I had known, comparing her to the woman now before me. Yes, Madeline was no longer eighteen. If my simple math was correct, she was thirty-five—the same age as me—and even more beautiful than I remembered.

A notable difference now was the amount of makeup she wore. It was too much for my liking. Seeing that didn't cause me to turn away. On the contrary, it flamed a desire deep within me to strip her of each layer until I was privy to the true beauty beneath.

Taking a sip of the bourbon remaining within my tumbler, I allowed my mind to fantasize about removing more than her makeup. First would be her silver strapless dress with a neckline that plunged between her round breasts. Each time she contemplated her next move, those same breasts pushed against the fabric as her breathing deepened.

Yes, I'd noticed.

While the pressure against the round globes was sexy as hell, it was also too regulated, too predictable. Even the way she tugged at her brightly painted red lip was practiced and perfected.

A hint of a smile came to my lips.

Yes, Madeline, I see the real you.

Once a con, always a con.

It seemed that now instead of taking advantage of tourists' naïveté by picking pockets or stealing apples on the crowded streets of Chicago, Madeline had moved on to stealing people's money in plain sight. A twinge of pride came over me as I observed her progress. There was no doubt that her current targets had more to lose.

Who was I to judge?

My pulse quickened as Madeline folded her cards, smiling at the dealer and the other players. The man behind her helped her with her chair as she stood. I knew from his uniform that he wasn't with her. He worked for the club. His job was to oversee her chips until she returned. She whispered something to him, handing him one of her poker chips—a $1000 tip.

He responded with a nod.

There was showmanship in each move by these high rollers.

Downing the rest of the bourbon, I handed the crystal tumbler to an attentive waitress.

"Mr. Kelly, may I get you another?"

I barely noticed the girl before me. My sights were set on only one woman as my pulse beat in triple time with anticipation. It had been too long.

"Sir?"

I turned toward the purple-haired young woman with the tray. "No, thank you."

My final sentiments weren't spoken aloud. They were waiting for the appropriate audience. *After all this time, I'm on my way to speak to my wife.*

MADELINE

Standing, I scanned the room, trying to shake the feeling that I was being watched. I didn't simply mean like every other poker player in the room. Of course we were being watched. A club providing this level of play had security. There were people watching the players and the dealers. It was big business and if word got out that Club Regal allowed cheating, the players would go somewhere else and take their money with them.

Each of the seven tables was filled with six players and one dealer. There were a few other patrons in the room, no doubt Chicago's elite. No one else would make it to this floor, much less through the door. Most of the nonplayers seemed preoccupied. This was the first night of the tournament, and there were too many tables and players to be interesting to observers.

By tomorrow night the tournament would be reduced to five

tables and thirty participants. Saturday afternoon, the five tables would be reduced to three. Come Saturday night, one table and six players would remain. That was why I was here, to be among the six elite players, the six vying for the million-dollar purse.

"Ms. Miller, your seat will be waiting," the gentleman who was watching our table said.

I handed him one of my chips. "Thank you. This is for your trouble. I'll be right back."

Looking at the tip in his hand, his smile broadened as he gave me a nod.

The young girl who'd once lived on these streets would never have comprehended a $1000 tip. That girl was gone.

A $1000 tip would guarantee my chips remained untouched until I returned.

Though I'd never been to Club Regal before, I'd been to many similar establishments. There was no denying the ambience around me. The atmosphere dripped with wealth. In my experience, many similar clubs had lost their old-time charm, giving way to a more modern appearance and atmosphere. In comparison to here, the others were sterile.

Club Regal was famous for the amenities upon the main floor: an exclusive steak house, the Bar Regal, and the Regal Cigar Room. Nothing but the best was stocked for the members. Those elite members of Club Regal no doubt believed themselves to be above others in this city; however, even with that status, not every member made it to the upper level and to this room. The conference room housing the poker tournament had been graced with the likes of movie stars and royalty as well as kingpins.

This was an establishment where old money talked, and new money was also heard.

It took connections and/or a reputation to be here.

My reputation was my ticket.

I'd played the circuits, working my way up to the elite poker tournaments. Over the years, I'd sat across the table from some of the world's best players. Kings and sheiks have folded with my bluffs. Of course, they don't know that.

A girl didn't bluff and tell.

As I made my way between the widely spaced tables and my high heels plunged into the plush carpet, I found myself admiring the rich dark paneling, custom molding, and heavy ornate light fixtures. If either were still alive, I wouldn't be surprised to see Al Capone or John Dillinger at one of the tables.

I would bet my life they graced this room and establishment at one time with their presence.

And placing bets was what I did.

Winning those bets was my livelihood, my repayment of debt.

With each step, I scanned the room looking for familiar faces at the various tables. It wasn't unusual for paths to cross. Derek Daniels and Lindsey Bolton were two I recognized. If conceit were a threat, I'd be worried.

It wasn't and neither was I.

Across the room I caught a glimpse of Julius Dunn. The man loved his picture on the cover of magazines. He didn't give a shit if it were *Forbes* or *The Sun*. He was of the belief that any publicity was good publicity. Most of the articles told of his partying and sexual exploits. If I were to accurately recall, he was on wife six or maybe waiting for seven.

My neck straightened at the sight of Marion Elliott. At nearly twice my age, he had been a part of the elite circuit since before I found my calling. His money came from big oil and like a bottomless well, he always came to a tournament with an unlimited supply of capital. Fate had been generous, keeping us from ever going head-to-head. If I were to win the jackpot, that would have to change. Of anyone in the room, he was my biggest concern.

I nodded to a gentleman near the exit, and he returned my nod with his own as he opened the door for my passage. Both sides of the entry were guarded, allowing only the appropriate clientele within. Even making it to this floor didn't guarantee entry into the high-roller lounge.

Despite my reputation and success, there was always a small twinge of irrational fear that upon my return, my inclusion would be blocked—the world would see me as the homeless street urchin I had once been in the shadows of this city.

Just as quickly, I pushed the thought away. Straightening my neck and squaring my shoulders, I reminded myself as well as the world that that girl was gone.

I'd come a long way since then.

Chicago was full circle for me, where I'd been born, lived, lost, survived, and where my life took an unexpected detour.

To say I'd escaped wouldn't be completely accurate. However, each victory and each win brought me closer to that dream. Stepping into the large landing, I took a deep breath of the cooler air. Step by step, I made my way through the maze of less crowded hallways on my way to my destination. It was obvious that few women made it to this floor; the ladies' room was less accessible.

I began to think about the cards. Perhaps it was returning to Chicago that had me off my game. I shouldn't have lost the last hand and I knew it. The city and its once familiar sights were affecting me in a way I couldn't describe.

My mind was on the last hand—one jack of diamonds away from an inside straight flush. The last raise would have been an uncalculated risk. I had more hands to play and more opportunities.

My lack of focus was a rookie mistake, one I rarely made.

I didn't see him until it was too late, until I turned the last corner to the isolated hallway that contained my destination.

A large hand surrounded my throat as my shoulders crashed against the wall. I struggled for breath as I was lifted until only the toes of my high-heeled shoes connected with the ground. The stench of liquor, no doubt expensive, prefaced his words as his dark, maleficent eyes stared into my own and his gravelly voice growled.

"You're down thirty grand."

This wasn't a random assault. I was well aware of my attacker.

Incapable of speaking, I blinked my response as moisture filled my eyes. Struggling for air, I lifted my hands to the one of his at my neck.

Mitchell Leonardo was correct; I was down. While most of my losses had been deliberate, I also had plans to rectify the situation. None of that mattered at this moment. My first objective was literally at hand.

I needed air—oxygen to my lungs, blood, and organs.

With the finals two days away, now was the time to create a facade, lull the other players into a false sense of assurance.

Mitchell should know that I wouldn't lose more than was allowed. I couldn't. There was too much riding on my success.

"Bitch, you know what will happen to both of us," he snarled with his lips near my ear, "if you don't win."

My freshly painted nails clawed at his grip of my neck as dark spots danced in my vision. Suddenly, his fingers released their hold. The rush of air was like a blowtorch shooting fire to my lungs. I leaned forward gasping, my knees weak.

"Stand up now or you won't be walking back in there."

With the fresh air bringing life back to my body and mind, I did as Mitchell said and straightened my stance. Our eyes again met. Instead of mine staring back at him with fear as he'd probably expected, fire and hate radiated from my gaze. My tone lowered as my inflection grew stronger with each word. "You son of a bitch, if you ever touch me again, you're a dead man and you won't be walking."

"You lose the boss's money, and I won't be the one six feet under."

"I'm working for the long haul, you idiot." I straightened my shoulders as I continued my stare into his dark orbs. "I realize you didn't land this babysitting job because of your brains, so let me dumb it down for you. Those people in there, they are a hell of a lot smarter than the likes of you. They've heard of my reputation. They're testing me. I know what the fuck I'm doing."

Mitchell's lips thinned, forming a straight line.

"The final games are in two days," I went on. "Losing now will increase the chances that the other players will underestimate me then. I'm also well aware of how much I need to win to secure my seating for each round." I separated my words as my determination built. "I have no doubt that I will not only make the final round but also win the jackpot on Saturday, and when I do, the first thing I'll tell Andros is what you just did. Untouchable. Does that sound familiar?" A menacing smile came to my lips as my head tilted coyly. "Or better yet, I'll ask him for a favor. You see, he's quite generous when I bring him winnings. He'll willingly give me my heart's desire."

"Watch yourself."

"Go make a phone call. Say goodbye to your unfortunate wife —my favor will make her a widow." I forced a chuckle as I eyed him up and down. "Hell, she'll probably thank me."

Mitchell bristled as he took a step back. "Doing my job, Ms. Miller. Watching you. Watching the boss's money."

"Glorified babysitter. Such a high-ranking job. Your momma must be proud." When Mitchell didn't respond, I continued. "You're watching me, then fucking *watch*." I pointed his direction, emphasizing my words. "You have put your hands on me for the last time. Do it again and I won't wait for Andros. I'll kill you myself."

With my last word, I stepped to the side and with a turn, disappeared into the ladies' bathroom. As the door successfully shut, I let out a long breath. Closing my eyes, I collapsed against the cool tile wall.

Mitchell was right about Andros's expectations.

Failure wasn't an option. The stakes were too high.

Taking a deep breath, I stepped to the mirror. Trailing my fingertips over my neck I lifted my chin and inspected the now-sensitive flesh.

"Stupid animal," I muttered as I opened my purse and

removed a small compact. A few dabs of powdered concealer and the red marks created by Mitchell's attempt at intimidation were disguised. Experience told me that the tenderness wouldn't be as easily hidden. I excelled at many things. Life was a brutal teacher. Hiding bruises was child's play, an elementary education. If life were a university, I would have PhD after my name.

Leaning forward, I ran another fingertip over my left cheek. The color beneath the layers of concealer and foundation was green to pale yellow. In other words, that bruise beneath was mostly healed. That beauty hadn't come from Mitchell but Andros himself, a reminder of who was in charge, who held my secrets, and who made decisions. After so many years outside of Chicago, I'd made the mistake of replying with honesty when he'd informed me of this job.

I didn't want to be here.

I would go anywhere else.

My finger skirted my bruised cheek.

I lowered my voice. "Fuckers. I'm biding my time. It won't be long until I will take what is mine and walk away."

My sentiment wasn't a child's wish for a new life such as the fairy tales and lies I was told before my family was taken from me. I knew that a knight on a white horse didn't exist and waiting for Prince Charming was a waste of time.

The only person who would save me was me.

One day I would.

I straightened my shoulders and stared into my own eyes.

Today wasn't the day. It wasn't a risk worth taking.

My priorities were set in stone.

Some things were worth a life sentence. I'd serve it. Nevertheless, I maintained hope for eventual parole. Forcing a smile in the mirror, I told myself it would come with either good behavior or really bad. Freedom earned or freedom stolen. I didn't care.

Andros owned my secrets but thankfully, not my heart. For the last five or more years, my body had also been out of his grasp. The kingpin of the Ivanov bratva—the Russian brotherhood—and I had come to a mutual understanding.

My stomach twisted.

Despite that agreement, I was still his, making me untouchable by the others in the bratva. At the same time, he was free to do as he desired with other women. Truthfully, I believed he grew bored of me yet refused to relinquish what he'd obtained. The new arrangement was the best one yet. However, as in all arrangement negotiations, everything could change on a dime. With Andros and the Ivanov bratva, a dime was a valueless example.

A kilo of cocaine.

A shipment of methamphetamine, heroin, or the newest street favorite, oxycodone.

A million-dollar payment.

An illegal shipment of guns.

The Ivanov world was located on the border of Canada, within the city of Detroit. Possibilities were endless. The shipping lanes in and out of the country were the gateway to wealth and power.

Lifting my chin in the mirror, I let out a breath and stared into my own green gaze.

Tonight I would concentrate on the next hour of poker, and then I could rest.

Opening the door to the hallway, my feet stilled as I gasped.

The view before me I'd last seen in my dreams.

I reached forward. Under my touch was a beating heart, its warmth radiating heat like flames from a campfire.

Shit.

This wasn't a dream or a ghost.

PATRICK

*H*er green eyes opened wide and her steps stuttered as her delicate hand came to my chest. The touch instantly combusted, flaring from sparks to flames. Madeline too must have felt it, for just as quickly, she pulled her hand away.

My tone lowered. "Mrs. Kelly, it's been a while. Welcome back to Chicago."

Madeline's chin rose. "That's not my name. Perhaps you have me confused with someone else."

Her visceral reaction didn't match her verbal response. Madeline was a gambler, but when she saw me, her mask shattered. Despite her attempt to appear indifferent, her body was giving her away. Her quickening breaths, parting lips, and flaring nostrils were but a few of the giveaways.

God, she was stunning.

There was no doubt in my mind.

It may have been seventeen years since I last laid eyes upon her, but I knew the only woman to take my name and my heart.

I wasn't wrong.

My body knew it as much as my mind.

A small grin came to my lips as I took her in, scanning from her shiny black hair all the way to her high-heeled shoes. No longer a child, Madeline Kelly was everything I remembered and more. Standing like the queen I'd always thought her to be, her shoulders were back and her neck was straight. The seductive scent of her perfume floated around her in a subtle cloud. Like the countryside after a rain, it brought me images of flowers near a cottage. Her dress was luxurious, possibly a designer original, and the way it accentuated her breasts made me want to rip it from her curves. The shoes upon her feet were no doubt high-end. Diamonds dripped from her ears and she was wearing more makeup than I preferred. Nevertheless, under the expensive wrapping, she was definitely the woman I remembered.

She was my wife.

As the mounting silence magnified around us, the need to reconfirm that this woman was flesh and blood and not an apparition created in my mind was intensifying by the minute. My hand itched to reach out. If her one-millisecond touch had surged like it had, doing more would be my downfall.

Being here with her was surreal, a dream or maybe a nightmare.

It was time to figure out which.

"If you'll excuse me," she said, breaking the silence as her eyes darted down the length of the hallway.

Unable to stop myself, I reached for her hand.

Such as it had been a moment earlier, the connection was instantaneous—like a jolt of electricity, it energized my dead heart. From the look in her eyes, I knew Madeline felt it too.

They were staring up at me, swirling with emotion. My finger went to her wrist. With one touch I felt her pulse. Similar to the one thundering through my veins, hers too was thumping too fast.

I tugged her forward, out into the empty hallway. "Don't worry, Madeline, we won't be disturbed if that's your concern." I shrugged. "Your friend is preoccupied."

She pulled her hand away, more than likely aware that our connection was one of her tells. Her profession made her wary, unwilling to show her cards.

As for her friend—the big man—I'd reached this hallway too late to intervene. And while I wasn't certain of all that had occurred, my gut told me that he might be a problem. A quick word to a friend, and the large man who had been talking with Madeline was now on the ground floor as his references for entry were being questioned. Depending upon his answers, reentry to this floor or maybe the club may be refused.

"My friend?" she asked. "My concern?" Her head shook as her long hair swayed like a black veil over her bare shoulders and down her back. "He's not a friend and my concern is the poker tournament. You'll have to excuse me now. I have more hands to play."

"You're mistaken. I don't have to do anything, especially excusing you from my sight. You are the one who came back to Chicago. Didn't you think it would be appropriate to alert your husband?"

"I'm not married."

"But you are, Maddie. You're married to me."

A smile graced her painted lips yet didn't make it to her emerald eyes. While the expression usually displayed pleasure, on her I saw sadness. "Maddie," she said wistfully. "No one calls me that, not anymore."

"My Maddie girl, our marriage was never dissolved. We were never divorced. Any other marriages that may have since occurred would be considered polygamy and most likely, give me license to murder."

Her eyes opened wide at my final comment before she replied, "There have been no others. No need for murder."

I wasn't certain about murder. It hadn't been ruled out. Nevertheless, I concentrated on her first sentence as I felt my cheeks rise. "No others...only one."

She let out an exaggerated breath. "Yes. But we both know it wasn't real. You know that. I know that. Sixteen years confirms that."

"Seventeen, Maddie," I corrected. "Seventeen. It was a cold winter day, just like today." I tried to recall. "Hell, it was January. We signed the license and promised forever before a judge. Real is a subjective qualifier. Legal isn't. Our marriage was as legal as if we'd said the words in a church. We missed celebrating our anniversary by a few weeks."

"All of them," she replied. "It doesn't matter. I can't think about any of this. I need to get back to the tournament."

My neck straightened. "And I need answers."

"You deserve them," she said. "You do. But quite honestly, I don't have any that are sufficient." She again lifted her petite hand to my chest. "You were a good man, Patrick Kelly. My name is now Miller. The girl you married never existed."

I'd married Madeline Tate. She may have ceased to exist, but she was obviously still alive.

Looking down at her hand, I took in her empty ring finger.

Covering her hand with mine, I marveled, if for only a moment, at the reality of her presence. "Do you feel it?" I asked.

Her chin rose until our gazes met. Beyond the expensive wrapping I saw the woman I'd married. She was buried beneath years of something I couldn't identify, but in the sparkle of her green eyes, I saw her.

"Feel what?" she asked.

"My heart."

She tried to pull her hand away, but I wouldn't release it.

"Patrick, I'm—"

"No," my tone lowered as I shook my head and leaned closer. "You fucking broke it the day you disappeared. Shattered it into a million pieces. Now you're back from the dead. I don't give a fuck about anything that has happened in the last seventeen years. Having you here right now..." My mind and body were at odds at having her close. "It makes me..." I didn't finish the sentence.

"What?" she asked. "It makes you what?

"I don't know. I either want to kill you or fuck you. I suppose the jury is still out."

Madeline let out a small feigned laugh. "You always have been brutally honest."

"I'm honest. My wife is right here and my intentions are unclear. I don't know what happened and why you left. I searched and searched. No one had answers. The only assumption I could make was that you were deceased. And yet here you are."

"And soon I'll be gone again," she said.

"To where?"

"To where I belong."

She retrieved the hand I'd held captive. "I must get back to the tournament. If I don't, I won't make the cut for tomorrow."

I took a step back. "Tonight, after the tournament, we will see one another again. That isn't a request."

"It would be better—"

"You yourself said that you owe me."

Her face tilted. "Perhaps I should know your intentions. Are you planning to kill me or fuck me?"

As I'd said, the jury was out. I'd never wanted both so badly in my whole life. Instead of answering, I asked, "Where are you staying?"

"You didn't answer my question." When I didn't respond, Madeline opened her purse and handed me a keycard. "Palmer House."

The white card had the hotel's emblem, but nothing else. "Room number?" I asked.

"Find me and then we can decide what the night will bring."

MADELINE

*a*s the final hand ended, I scooped in the winnings and took inventory of my chips. At the end of play, I was down close to ten grand. And despite my mind being all kinds of mixed up, down ten meant I'd recovered $20,000 since seeing Patrick. It should be enough to guarantee my return to play tomorrow night.

The dealers were making their final count of wins and losses. The entire room waited with bated breath for the names of those who advanced to be announced.

Forty-two players began play earlier in the evening.

Twelve players would be eliminated.

It couldn't be me.

By my estimation I'd made a healthy recovery, bringing my holdings back to near forty grand. I couldn't be certain of the other tables and had purposely tried to stay in the middle of the rankings. Too high or too low would bring more attention. That was never my goal.

I believed once it was all said and done, I'd end up in the top eighteen to twenty-second seating. Of course, a miscalculation could place me a bit lower. I fought the onset of nerves, convincing myself that I was mostly confident I'd made the advancing thirty. The truth was that I was as confident as I could be since sighting Patrick—since that meeting, I was unsure of most everything.

Making the cut wasn't an option. I had to be there.

"Ladies and gentlemen," the announcer spoke as the room quieted, "while it's unusual, we have received word of a buy-in for the continuation of the tournament. Mr. Hillman, Mr. Antonio Hillman, was unable to attend tonight. His contribution secured his seat for tomorrow. With him in thirtieth position, we will now announce the other twenty-nine players in ascending order."

The room around me filled with gasps of disbelief as we looked to one another, shaking our heads and pursing our lips. While it was true that we'd all bought our way into the tournament, it wasn't for the second round.

Hillman.

I wasn't sure why the name was familiar.

I recognized it, but for some reason I didn't think it was from poker.

Then why would it sound familiar?

My neck straightened and skin prickled as I waited to hear my name.

The announcer began with the top ranking: Marion Elliott. The room broke out into applause. While I played the role, clapping my hands and smiling, my empty stomach twisted, churning the bile that comes without eating. If I were to win the jackpot, I would need to face him. The prospect terrified me like no other player.

I couldn't let myself think that way.

Fucking with people's minds before the first card was dealt was the sign of a true champion.

Two, three, and four, the names continued to be announced. As we all waited, I made eye contact with Mitchell. My bodyguard-slash-babysitter was standing along the far wall with a glass of bourbon in his hand and my winter coat draped over his arm. I wasn't certain where he'd been, but at least he was back.

"Nineteen: Madeline Miller."

I let out a breath and gazed at Mitchell who nodded.

Antonio Hillman was announced at number thirty. He'd bought his way to the bottom of the rankings. I scoured the room wondering who had metaphorically paid the price for his entry.

Who was cut because of his buy-in?

The room was beginning to empty. If I wanted a visible reaction from one or more of the players, I was watching the wrong crowd. Poker players on this level knew how to hide their true feelings.

Tucking the receipt for my chips into my handbag, I began to stand. As I did, Mitchell came my way and helped me with my chair. "I will escort you to your hotel room. Then I need to do some work for the boss. There are a few things he wants me to check out." Once I stood, Mitchell offered me my coat and added, "You're fucking lucky you made the cut."

My head shook. "Thank you, Mitchell, for your vote of confidence." My eyebrows lifted. "And for your information, it wasn't luck. The word is skill." I tilted my head. "Where have you been?"

"None of your concern."

Together we walked down the grand stairs.

My steps stuttered when I saw Marion Elliott standing at the bottom of the staircase, his hand on the banister and a grin on his wrinkled face. Heat filled my cheeks. Surely he wasn't waiting for me.

"Ms. Miller," he said, his Texas drawl coating the greeting in sweet molasses.

Mitchell's dark eyes came my way, but my attention went to the man who'd just addressed me. "Mr. Elliott."

He offered me his hand for the last step. "Please, call me Marion." He bent gallantly at the waist and lightly kissed the knuckles of my hand in his grasp.

Retrieving my hand, I nodded. "Marion, it's very nice to finally meet you. I'm Madeline."

"My dear, of course I know who you are. I was elated to see your name on the lineup."

"You flatter me," I said. "Honestly, I'm surprised you know of me."

Mitchell respectively took a few steps away, allowing Marion and I a moment to talk.

"You are very well known," Marion replied. "Beautiful, mysterious, and lethal."

My head tilted. "An interesting description."

Marion gestured toward the bar. "I was hoping I could entice you to have a drink with me this evening."

"I'm sorry. It's late and my standing isn't as secured as yours. I need my rest before tomorrow."

"Tomorrow night then?"

"I thank you for the invitation."

"And I hope to see you across the table on Saturday night. It will make my weekend complete."

I forced a grin. "Time will tell."

"Ms. Miller?" Mitchell called. "I believe our taxi is waiting."

"I could offer you my driver—"

I lifted my hand, stopping his offer. "Thank you. Tomorrow."

Another gallant bow before his response, "Tomorrow it is."

We made our way to the front of the club, and Mitchell stepped up to a waiting taxi cab.

Despite the grand canopy over the entrance, the cold winter wind whipped around us. As we climbed into the taxi, it tousled my hair, making dark strands flutter around my face. When the door to the taxi closed, my entire body trembled as I smoothed my hair with my now-gloved hands.

I hated cold. It wasn't that Detroit—where I was living—was a mecca of tropical breezes and sunshine. It was more about knowing what it was like to be cold, really cold. I did and I didn't like any part of it.

Marion's offer of a drink and then his driver caused me to contemplate the taxi moving through the streets. There were times when Mitchell was more than my babysitter—he was also my driver. I was never told why in some locations we used public transportation and in others we didn't. It wasn't my job to question. That was something I'd been told enough to recite the phrase in my sleep.

My job was to do what I'd just done.

To win.

With Mitchell and me in the back seat, we continued to ride

through Chicago's late-night traffic. Around us, bright street lights projected circles of illumination onto the sidewalk as snow and sleet glistened in the air. Looking up, tall buildings loomed over us; even higher, names were lit at the top.

If I pretended to not know the Chicago of my past, I could possibly see the city for its beauty. Smaller than New York and larger than Detroit, Chicago had midwestern charm as well as a hint of the East Coast elite. However, seeing it that way and forgetting my past wasn't possible, not after tonight's encounter. Now, as I stared out of the taxi's windows, my gaze went beyond the circles of light and down alleyways too dark to see.

In my mind's eye, I saw what was otherwise invisible. I saw the world that visitors and even residents with warm homes and full bellies chose not to see. It was a world of makeshift housing, warmth coming from flames in a barrel, and hungry bellies. This time of year, most would do their best to find a roof and a bed off of the cold, hard ground. When missions and shelters reached capacity, abandoned buildings and underground train stations no longer part of the "L" were plausible gathering places for the invisible.

That was where Patrick and I first met.

Now that advancing in the tournament was secured, my mind went to where it had been trying to settle all night. It went to Patrick.

MADELINE

Hollywood and novels glamorized the life Patrick and I had shared in a way it didn't deserve. It wasn't romantic or adventurous. It was difficult and dangerous. However, no matter what memory came to mind concerning Patrick Kelly, I found it impossible to dislike the boy I knew. Together we survived. We picked pockets and scrounged for money and food.

There were easier paths that were available to us, selling drugs or maybe ourselves, but even in our hopeless dark world, while together we'd maintained a semblance of honor.

I opened my purse. Shaking my head, I silently berated myself for giving him the keycard. A man of honor was how I always wanted to remember him. The girl he'd loved was how I wanted to be remembered.

Would his visit to my room change that?
Would he visit?
The questions continued without answers.

Why had I agreed to return to Chicago?

Of all the places in the city, how had he found me?

"I don't see my keycard," I said aloud to Mitchell. It was the first we'd spoken since entering the taxi.

"What?"

"I think I lost it. It probably fell out one of the times I opened my purse."

"As long as you have the receipt for your chips, I don't give a shit about the keycard," Mitchell said. "There aren't numbers on the card for anyone to associate it with your room. We'll stop at the front desk and have someone make you a new one."

The taxi pulled up in front of the Palmer House.

As the door was opened, a new gust of cold wind infiltrated our warm bubble, and my body again trembled. While Mitchell paid the fare, I took the bellman's hand and with my high heels on the wet concrete, I stood. Rubbing my gloved hands together, I waited until Mitchell joined me so we could enter the lobby together.

"I can take care of the key," I volunteered.

"Boss's orders. I'm going with you."

My shadow. Maybe I could add that to my list of descriptors.

Babysitter.

Sometimes driver.

Shadow.

There was no sense arguing with Mitchell. It wasn't worth it. I would save my argument for any requests he made to enter my room. My nerves grew tauter with the unknown.

Would Patrick be waiting for me?

With even the slightest possibility of that, I couldn't allow my shadow's entrance.

"Hello," I said, speaking to the older gentleman behind the VIP desk. "I seem to have misplaced my keycard."

"Yes, Ms. Miller. May I see your ID?"

When I didn't respond, he went on, "Protocol, ma'am. We wouldn't want to grant anyone else entrance to your room."

I suppressed a grin and the small hairs on my arm bristled with his comment. Although, I wasn't one hundred percent certain, I did think that someone else in my room was exactly what I wanted.

"Let me get it for you," I said.

Opening my handbag, I retrieved my identification. As I handed it his direction, I glanced at the license and for the first time in many years, I thought about my name. Madeline Miller.

The person I'd become had the appropriate paper trail—license, passport, even a birth certificate. None of it was real. Truly, it was amazing what was possible with the right connections. Nevertheless, the truth remained: Madeline Miller wasn't a real person. She wasn't born in a small town to a stay-at-home mother and a factory worker father. She didn't lose her parents in a car accident nor not know her father's profession. She never had a house with a picket fence.

It made for a great biography: woman makes it big in the world of poker coming from grassroots beginnings.

I shook my head.

Patrick was right. Legally, my identification should say Madeline Kelly. Our marriage that really wasn't was never legally dissolved or ended. The only proof that our marriage occurred was an old piece of paper, if it still existed.

Would the courthouse still have a copy?

Would our marriage have seemed more real if I had changed my identification back then?

"Here you go, Ms. Miller," the gentleman said as he handed me the new keycard and my identification. "Have a good night."

Mitchell stepped forward, his usually gruff tenor sounding almost gentlemanly. "I assume room service is still available."

"Yes, sir. Until midnight."

As we stepped away, I asked, "Are you planning a dinner party in your room?"

He reached forward and pushed the *up* button near the elevators. "You are. Not a party, but you're not leaving your room until morning. Boss's orders."

My lips came together while a barrage of responses came to mind.

Yet as more people joined us within the confines of the elevator, I kept them all to myself. It wasn't until we were walking down the quiet hallway to my room that I stole a glance at the large man beside me, knowing I needed to keep him from entering my room, even if his only goal was to be certain it was clear.

Add bodyguard to the list.

Outside my room, I stopped. "Listen, Mitchell, I'm tired. I have two more days of this tournament and then we'll be gone from here. My plans for the evening include a bath and sleep. You don't need to babysit me any longer. Rest assured there's nowhere I want to be on this cold Chicago night. Roaming this hotel or the windy city in sub-zero temperatures isn't on my agenda."

"Boss told me to be sure you eat."

Why was it that Andros's concern made me feel like more of a trained pet than a person? Don't forget to feed the cat.

I shook my head at the demeaning comparison. "Fine, I'll add eating to my list of things to do."

"He doesn't want you to forget. I could bring you something from the restaurant and you won't need to call room service."

I wasn't confident of what had happened or caused the change from earlier, but Mitchell's demeanor had made a sudden improvement. Maybe it had to do with why he had gone missing for part of the evening. Or perhaps, Mitchell had been stupid enough to tell Andros how he'd tried to bully me. Maybe his change in attitude was due to the way I responded, not Andros. I couldn't be sure. It was another thing I was uncertain about.

One thing I did know was that Mitchell's least irritating quality was his lack of intelligence. Yes, he was a brute and at times, I wanted him six feet under, but he was also gullible. If I reported his behavior to Andros, there was no guarantee his replacement wouldn't be worse.

In this life, one took the bad with the good.

"Thank you. I'm good with room service," I replied. "Go to bed or do whatever you still need to do for Andros. I know you both have my phone monitored. I won't leave the room."

"The boss is..." He didn't finish. "He's concerned about this city. Don't do anything stupid."

I forced a feigned chuckle. "We both know it's too late for that, Mitchell."

Pushing away the weight of stupid decisions over my lifetime, I inserted the keycard. Anticipation was a strange feeling, hope and excitement balled up into one. Rarely had I felt it, and yet now I did.

Before entering the room, I turned back to Mitchell—in whatever role he was playing. "I'm in for the night. Your job is over until morning."

He nodded and began to walk away.

Holding my breath, I stepped inside and scanned the hotel room.

The drapes were drawn, lights on, and bed was turned down with the customary green mint on the pillow. I peered into the bathroom—empty. Slowly, I opened the closet doors. Except for my clothes, it too was empty.

Tears prickled my eyes as I collapsed on the edge of the bed, laid my purse on the nightstand, and fumbled with the large buttons on my coat. Disappointment was an emotion I recognized.

What had I expected, that Patrick would be waiting with wine and roses?

Standing, I shook droplets of melting snow from my coat and placing it on a hanger, returned it to the closet. Kicking off my high heels, I wiggled my toes into the carpeting. A tug to the side zipper on my dress, and the silver material pooled around my feet.

Stepping out of the dress, I reached for the robe.

While the unexpected disappointment at Patrick's absence nibbled at my consciousness, I slid my arms into the soft terry cloth and walked to the tall windows. Reaching for the draperies, I pulled one aside, as I stared out at the Chicago skyline sparkling through the frost.

Despite the thick thermal panes, a cold chill ran through me, cooling my circulation and dotting my skin with goose bumps.

Warding off the melancholy drop in temperature, I instinctively wrapped the robe tightly around me and secured the tie.

Lost in my own thoughts, the beep of the door's lock and sounds of mechanisms disengaging caught me off guard.

Spinning toward the door, my breath caught.

Without hesitation, the door opened inward.

MADELINE

"*O*h my God," I mumbled, unsure if it was meant as a plea or a surrender.

Patrick.

I reached for the lapels of the robe I'd just secured and tugged them closed, suddenly aware that beneath the soft terry cloth I wore only panties. The dress hadn't allowed for a bra.

At the sight of him, thoughts and feelings brewed within me. Each one brought life back to my mind and body. It was as if the energy he produced sparked through the air an electrical current capable of resuscitating the person I'd once been.

Despite how I'd responded at Club Regal, from the moment I opened the bathroom door, I knew exactly who he was. "Pat —" I began.

With a twist of his neck, Patrick's intense blue stare came over his wide shoulder. Without uttering a word, he silenced whatever I'd been about to say. The door behind him was now closed.

I tried to swallow as my mouth dried, watching as Patrick turned the deadbolt and fastened the chain. My pulse thumped through my veins seasoned with uncertain emotions swirling within that same circulation. We were locked in this room together, alone like we hadn't been in forever.

Never once had I been afraid of Patrick. Yet there was something different about him now versus the boy I recalled. This man, the one in my room, emanated power. It wasn't from anything he said or did. It radiated from his presence, a confidence that wasn't manufactured but instead, innate. In a way, as I stood there, I half expected to see the world around him blur from the aura.

Should I be afraid?

My thoughts were having difficulty concentrating on anything other than the fact that he was here. I was here. We were together.

The last time I'd heard about him, he'd left for the service—army, I thought.

It wasn't that he'd merely enlisted; I'd been told he'd gone to war, not the battles we'd fought as children, but the real war from which people never returned. After that news, I never attempted to confirm his whereabouts.

Perhaps I was afraid he hadn't returned.

None of that mattered any longer.

There was no longer a need for confirmation.

Patrick Kelly was here—in my hotel room—in all his manly glory.

My skin twitched as I fought the childish impulse to tug on my lip. It was a habit that I'd stopped long ago, the simple gesture revealed more than I wanted to show.

Insecurity.

Uncertainty.

Shame at decisions made.

Concern.

My thoughts were too many to articulate.

I concentrated not on what I thought or felt but on what I saw.

Oh, how he'd changed.

The man Patrick had become filled the hotel room's foyer.

His broad shoulders, trim waist, and long legs created an impassable mountain in my path. With the light shining from above, I could make him out even better than in the club's dimmer hallway. My gaze scanned from his blond hair—shorter than when we were young, his light blue eyes, and high cheekbones, to his defined, chiseled jaw and thick neck.

The painful twinge twisting within my chest conveyed what my eyes and mind couldn't comprehend. I sucked in a deep breath and with my pulse beating in double time, I forced my steps forward.

One and then another.

Patrick didn't move, speak, or even blink.

A statue in a designer suit, he could have been a Brooks Brothers mannequin in the way his jacket hung perfectly from his frame. The white shirt beneath was starched and crisp, disappearing beneath the trousers and black belt.

I came to a stop inches from his chest, unable to move closer. Now in my bare feet, I was a good ten or more inches shorter than him.

Had he always been as tall?

Stillness filled the hotel room with deafening silence.

Even the hum of the heat disappeared as his gaze moved from my head to my toes. With each passing second, my skin warmed, reminding me that under the robe I was nearly naked, preparing as I'd been for my impending bath. As we continued our silent battle of wills, my nipples drew tight and my core clenched.

It wasn't fear that Patrick's proximity instilled.

It was something else, something I'd forgotten.

It had been so long since I had a spontaneous physical reaction to a man that my body and mind were having difficulty processing. One would think this carnal reaction was not uncommon when faced with a handsome mountain of a man. But it was as I pondered this thought that I realized that neither of us had spoken. "Patrick, you found me."

"Oh, Madeline, finding you wasn't an issue. The question remains did I want to?" His head tilted, his handsome face taut as the cords in his neck pulled tight. "I don't have the answer to that yet."

The rich scent of his spicy cologne settling in the air filled my lungs, creating a magical concoction. As had been in the hallway at the club, we were again close. It would only take a small step for me to feel the firmness of his chest against mine. I peered upward. Without thinking, I allowed my hand to do what it had wanted to do at the club.

I laid my palm against his stubbly cheek. The prickling rekindled the connection I'd felt earlier. Like electricity, the connection tingled my palm. Looking up into his blue eyes, I said, "God, Patrick, I never thought I'd see you again or that you'd want to see me. It's been a lifetime."

That statement was more accurate than I could admit—the

life we'd shared and the one we hadn't. Half of one person's life was the whole of another's.

It would be easy to melt into him, to remember what we once had.

My hand lowered from his cheek to his chest. He moved closer, one step and then another. Our feet moved in unison until my back collided with the wall. All the while, our gazes never parted. I found myself mesmerized by the cyclone of emotions swirling within his blue orbs.

Without speaking, he reached for my waist and pulled me toward him.

No longer did I imagine the firmness of his chest against my breasts. It was there, solid as a statue and emitting heat.

"I found you, Maddie, now what am I going to do with you?"

There was an unfamiliar edge to his voice that set off my nerves.

Kill or fuck.

"Nothing," I said, doing my best to sound confident. "I'm here for the tournament. After that I'll leave."

Patrick's head shook as his finger skirted over the side of my face and down my neck. It was a ghost of a touch as if he were restraining himself. That thought made me want him to let go.

"I think it's more," he said. "I think after all this time, you came to my city to fuck with me." A forced grin came to his lips. "And now that we're here, I don't have a problem with that. As a matter of fact, right now, I want it too."

My mind was a blur as the proximity of his body and the hardening of his erection confirmed the accuracy of his intent. Yes, I was turned on. No, I wasn't prepared for more. I hadn't been with a man in over five years. The idea frightened me more than it excited me. My head shook. "No, Patrick. That's not why I'm here."

He took a small step back. "Are you saying you don't want to fuck?"

My neck straightened. "I'm saying...that isn't an option..."

"I believe you're mistaken. Fucking my wife again is an option, one I haven't had for a long time but now do." His finger again came to my cheek, neck, and down to my collarbone as he peered into the V of my robe. "You were always too beautiful." He lifted my chin. "It was a liability when we were young. Now I assume it is part of your arsenal." Before I could respond, he added, "Too much makeup but still stunning."

I lowered my chin to obstruct his view. "Come sit down. We can talk." When he didn't move, I placed more pressure against his chest and looked into his blue orbs. "You were a lot of things, Patrick Kelly, but you never forced me..." The words created a bubble in my throat I tried to swallow. I didn't want to think about nonconsensual sex.

"Really, Maddie? You didn't come to Chicago after all this time to fuck with my head? Because seeing you has done that, and being close to you makes me want to tug the tie on this robe and remember what it's like to get lost inside you. You've fucked with my thoughts. It's only fair I get my turn."

My neck stiffened. "I want you to leave."

"I want to fuck my wife. Either we both get our way or neither of us do."

My eyes closed slowly as I let out a breath. This wasn't what I wanted or imagined. To be honest, I wasn't certain of what I wanted. It seemed abundantly clear that the reunion I'd dared to dream about over the years wouldn't happen.

I should have known better. After all, I'd never been the happily-ever-after type of girl.

Happy endings and dreams were simply illusions our minds created to soften life's blows, an alternate universe that existed only in the realm of make-believe. Maybe for a moment while basking in the rich aroma of his cologne, I'd dared to entertain such a notion, but that was simply another mistake my mind made when it came to this man.

Hopes and dreams were the thoughts and illusions of little girls. That wasn't me. I wasn't certain it ever had been.

My shoulders straightened as I reached for his hand. "Let's talk. Tell me why you're really here."

His features hardened as he stepped away from my touch. "I think you should answer that question first."

PATRICK

*I*n the following seconds, Madeline's expression cooled. The genuineness of her gaze dimmed in her green orbs like cooling embers that were no longer privy to the flame. Whatever she'd been thinking a moment ago was disappearing behind a well-practiced mask.

Her chin lifted defiantly. "I've told you that I'm here for the poker tournament. I'm not sure why you came here, but if it's for any other reason, then you should go."

"You played the odds by inviting me to your room. Now I'm here. Isn't that what you do, gamble?"

"You think I gambled on you?"

I pulled the keycard from my pocket. "You gave me the key."

"I did. It was a mistake," she said with a shrug. "Maybe I wanted to see the boy I knew one more time."

Madeline brushed by me, the softness of the robe fluttering against my hand as she made her way toward a sofa near the windows. Catching her, I reached for her hand and spun her back around until we were again face-to-face. As she had been moments ago, her soft, supple body was against me, the beat of her heart hammering against my chest. My tone lowered as I stared down at her beauty. "The *boy* is gone and so is the girl. It's time to be the adults we once thought we were."

Her chin rose. "You're right, Patrick. Our rosy childhood is a thing of the past."

"I'm not leaving until I have answers." Releasing her hand, I stepped away. It was then I saw the dress she'd been wearing lying upon the carpet. I picked it up, noticing the softness of the material. I brought it to my nose. For a moment my eyes closed.

The material held her lingering scent covered in a sweet, perfumed fragrance. Fuck, the whiff alone brought my dick to life. "I've missed..." I didn't finish. There were too many options.

"This isn't..." Madeline stopped talking and spun in place as if trying to get her bearings.

I'd seen others make similar moves when cornered. Yet watching the gorgeous woman before me didn't give me the sense of a trapped animal; instead, it was as if she were drifting and in need of an anchor.

If after all this time, my wife was a ship lost at sea, I had to admit, if only to myself, I was fucking thrilled she'd made it back to my harbor. Tossing the dress on the bed, I reached for her again. She came to a stop, her green stare upon me. "Maddie."

Her lids fluttered momentarily. "I've missed that name. I've missed hearing it from you."

My hands went to her cheeks. "Everything."

"Everything?"

"I've missed every fucking thing about you. I never allowed

myself to do it, but now, here, fuck, it's like a landslide of memories—the way you slept, smiled, smelled, and tasted."

It was a fucking pull I couldn't control—an unbreakable twenty-ton chain bringing us together. The cogs were turning ever slowly, link by link. With the sound of her breaths in my ears, I leaned closer and brought my lips to hers.

I expected Madeline to resist by pulling away, or perhaps slapping me and telling me to stop.

Not just expected...I needed her to do that, to be the one to stop what I couldn't.

However, as our kiss deepened, her breasts pressed harder against me, her soft moans filled my ears, and my tongue invaded the sweet warmth of her lips, I knew without a doubt that her return would ruin us. My body and mind were on a collision course to our mutual destruction. If I didn't stop, I never would.

I lowered my touch, skirting her arm, until my fingers found hers, intertwining as they once had. I held on to her. Like the young boy leading the girl through the dark alleyways, I wanted to lead her away from here to a place where we could reconnect.

Breaking our kiss, I lifted her hand in mine. It was her left hand. The fourth finger was bare, as it had been seventeen years ago. A ring was another expense we promised to someday afford. I brought her knuckles to my lips and after leaving a kiss, I looked up. "Whether you admit it or not, we are still married and without a doubt, you are fucking with me."

"Do you still want to kill me?"

"Not as badly as I want to fuck you."

Her breathing deepened and nostrils flared as the spark I remembered glistened in her gaze. "I haven't wanted that in so long, I'd forgotten what it felt like."

"And now?"

"Patrick, I can't tell you...almost anything. I can tell you that it's been forever since I felt safe with a man. I feel that way with you even after all these years."

Indescribable desire such as I couldn't recall percolated within me. My hands longed to roam her soft skin. My arms ached to hold her. My hardened dick grew painful. My gaze simmered on hers. "Don't fool yourself, Maddie. You're not safe with me. I want answers from you, but fuck. If I don't rein this in, I don't think I can stop."

"Do you want to stop?"

Hell no.

"I didn't come here for this."

"So you came to kill me?" By the sparkle in her eyes and the upturn of her lips she knew that wasn't the case.

"I came to get answers." My breathing stopped as Maddie reached for the hem of her robe.

"I have one answer I can show you. It's all I have."

I couldn't look away.

She reached beneath the length of the robe and lowered a pair of silver panties until they fell to the floor and she stepped away.

"You seem to be losing your clothes to the floor. Your dress and now..." My words stilled as she tugged on the sash and opened the robe. Inch by inch, I took in her natural beauty, her curves, including the roundness of her breasts, fuller than they'd been when we were young. My gaze lowered to the flatness of her stomach and the trimmed patch of dark hair, curlier than those on her head. I could hardly breathe as she added the robe to the floor's collection and turned away.

Her ass was round and perfect, and on her left cheek was a small tattoo.

She craned her neck back at me. "You're the only person on this earth who knows the meaning of that tattoo."

I took a step closer, and as I did, she reached down to retrieve the robe.

"Don't you fucking dare."

"Patrick. I just—"

"No." I reached for her waist and pulled her ass toward me as I stared at the small red apple tattooed on the flesh of her ass cheek.

Our first meeting came back in a wave of emotion.

The apple.

The policemen.

The chase.

I ran the tip of my finger over the artwork.

Fucking soft as a baby's butt.

A gasp filled the room as goose flesh came to life over her skin.

Madeline wasn't a baby. She was all woman, bared naked within my grasp.

Without thinking, my hand came back, palm straightened, and I swung it forward, landing my palm on her ass. My hand tingled as her ass cheek reddened, the skin matching the apple.

"Fuck, Patrick." Leaning forward, her hands landed on the window's glass as she let out a squeal.

"That's for me. You marked yourself for me. Now it's my turn."

Madeline sighed. "No one else knows what it means."

"It means you're mine." I looked at her delicate hands splayed on the glass. "Don't fucking let go of that window."

Her face turned toward the glass. "What if someone sees?"

"We're twenty stories in the air." I brushed her long hair to one side. Reaching for her hips, I pulled her ass against my hardened erection. Leaning over her back, I whispered menacingly in her ear, purposely exhaling warm air on the sensitive skin of her neck. "I wish the whole damn world could see, see you, see us, see that damn apple, and see that you're mine."

"I-I..."

"Can you feel how hard I am?" I hadn't been this hard for any woman since her. It was another of the things I tried to forget. Grinding her ass over my trousers was positively painful. If I didn't get inside her soon, I might react more like a teenager than the man I was. "I didn't come here to fuck you, but I'm going to."

"It's been a long..." Her voice cracked. "I'm scared."

With one hand still holding her hip, I unbuckled my belt, lowered the zipper, and freed myself from my boxer briefs. My heavy cock sprang outward. Taking it in hand, I ran my grip up and down. With each stroke I grew impossibly harder, going from erect to steel.

"Tell me no," I said, running my hand again over her ass.

"I don't know."

Lowering my touch, I found my home, the only place I'd wanted to stay. "Spread your legs, Maddie girl. If you're not wet, I will turn around and walk away. If you are, I'm reclaiming what's mine."

MADELINE

"... *If* you are, I'm reclaiming what's mine."

Each word struck me to the core as his warm breath sent chills tingling down my spine. My feet moved apart, doing as he'd said. It was the moment of truth, one that despite my rekindled desire, I feared I'd fail.

Wet.

I hadn't been wet since I could recall.

Gels worked to make sex less painful.

Orgasms happened or they didn't.

Spontaneous arousal wasn't something I could control.

And yet having Patrick's hands on me awakened something that was both stimulating and vaguely familiar. I fidgeted as his hands continued to roam over my skin. Strong and forceful, yet tender—it was a masterful combination that I'd never known with anyone but Patrick.

Now it was more.

"I'm not..." My sentence faded into the cloud of lust and desire. There were so many sensations that I found myself yearning.

Could it be?

Maybe.

Yes.

With my breasts heavy and my nipples hard, I was aroused. The heat of his touch bubbled within me, making me want what I hadn't for so long. The need wasn't only physical. I wanted that, for him to take me. It was more. It was emotional. I wanted to remember what it had been like to be with someone I trusted, someone I'd loved.

Even if it was in the past.

My neck craned to the side, allowing me to catch a glimpse of the handsome man behind me. His eyes were wide, staring down at my ass and the apple I'd had inked a lifetime ago. From my angle, I saw his strained neck, white shirt, and suit coat. My gaze went to my bare feet. On either side was a large black loafer.

Oh my God.

He was going to fuck me. I was naked and he was still fully dressed.

I don't know what made that so hot, but it was.

My core clenched as Patrick's touch moved to my entrance.

"Gah..." I sighed as one and then two of his long fingers slid within me.

"You're wet, Maddie girl. Your body wants this. Tell me to stop."

His hand had created a rhythm as his fingers curled.

Shamelessly, my knees bent as I moved with him. It was as his thumb found my clit that I froze. Like the shock of electricity from our first touch, he already had me on the edge.

"Tell me," Patrick growled near my ear.

Like a log jam made up of too much to process and unable to move, for a moment my answer stuck in my throat. His fingers again moved, commanding my attention and filling my circulation with both endorphins and wonder.

I was wet.

I was aroused.

And I wanted this more than I'd wanted any man since him. Breaking free, the words came out like rapid-fire. "Don't stop. Oh, please don't stop."

As if not hearing me, his fingers disappeared. And all at once, we were one.

My back arched as a scream tore from my throat, echoing around us.

Oh God. It was good, yet so much more than I recalled.

"Fuck yes," his deep baritone approval washed over me.

Patrick's speed slowed as he continued his claim. My scarred core fought the stretch. I bit my lip as I willed his entrance. Bit by bit, he did what I thought was impossible, going deeper and deeper until he stilled.

"They say we build things up in our mind," he said as his warm breath skirted over my neck and collarbone, bringing goose bumps to my exposed flesh. "...that our memories exaggerate reality. That's not true. Being here right now, with you, within you, you're...it's better than I remember. Maddie, it's fucking heaven."

My breasts heaved as I panted heated breaths, covering the glass with fog. The only clarity was where my splayed fingers flexed upon the slippery window. I lifted my face to the glass. Within the condensation, I was able to see the reflection of the handsome man behind me. I found my voice. "Don't stop. Remind me what it's like to be with my husband."

His grip of my hips intensified as he thrust faster, creating sensations cascading from my core to my toes. It was a cyclone of feelings, building higher and higher until every nerve all the way to my scalp tingled. The room filled with noises and sounds of pleasure as my nerves grew taut. I was on a cliff, twenty stories in the air.

The cars and lights twinkled below.

This wasn't like I remembered sex with Patrick. It was more.

He wasn't a seventeen- or eighteen-year-old boy anymore. Patrick was a man.

Relentlessly, he took, pounding into me, with his strong fingers gripping and bruising with their possessive hold.

I couldn't last any longer.

My toes curled, and I jumped into the air. Hell no. It wasn't a jump but a fall. "Patrick," I called out as the fireworks exploded and I leaned into the wind, riding the current in a free fall to the ground below.

As our connection severed, my muscles lost their battle. Yet before I hit the ground, Patrick's strong arms lifted me, cradling me to his chest. After a kiss to my hair, he turned and laid me upon the bed.

"For the record, that wasn't what it's like to be with your husband. That was what it was like to be fucked, to be reclaimed."

I lifted my shoulders and head as I put my weight on my elbows. The tips of my lips moved upward as my gaze stayed fixed on him, his suit still in place with only his trousers undone displaying his shiny large still-erect cock.

The thought regarding the lack of condom came and went. Pregnancy wasn't an issue, and I knew I was clean. At the moment, as he stalked toward me, there were more pressing matters.

"Can you remind me?" I asked.

"No," he said as he kicked off his shoes, shed his suit coat, shirt, trousers, and finally his boxer briefs.

The striptease had me momentarily distracted. "You can't remind me what it was like?"

His large body caused the mattress to dip as he sat beside me in all his nude glory. "No, Madeline." He smoothed a rogue strand of my hair away from my face. "I'm not going to make love like a married man. I don't even know what the hell that means. I never got the chance to fall into that routine." His finger trailed over my collarbone and down to the dip between my breasts.

I startled as his lips came down on one nipple and his fingers tweaked the other. A jolt of lightning zapped through me. Licks and nips alternated from side to side.

When he looked back up, there was a smile on his face. "I am a married man. Don't forget it. I'm married, to you. I hadn't planned on spending tonight fucking."

"That makes two of us," I said with a weary grin as his touch roamed over my skin.

"But now that I have you here, I can't stop. Tomorrow when you walk, sit, or even fucking stand still, I want you to feel me, to know that I was where I belong. I want you to think about everything I did to you. Every way you came until you couldn't come again. Mrs. Kelly, I want you to admit that you belong with me."

His words enticed and saddened me. Tonight was a mistake. Forever was impossible. "Patrick, I can't—"

Patrick's finger came to my lips. "No, Maddie. Not tonight. I see it. I know you."

My head shook. "See what? You don't know me. Not anymore."

"I know something just made you sad. I saw it in your eyes. There were clouds. Push them away."

"But—"

"No more talking," he interrupted. "I need answers. I want answers. You fucking owe me answers, but not tonight. Tonight I'm fucking my wife—seventeen years' worth."

My eyes opened wide.

Holy shit.

If he were serious, tomorrow I not only wouldn't move without remembering him, I wouldn't move. Period.

Patrick reached for my ankles and shifted each leg, leaving my knees bent and feet apart.

A chill settled over me as I tried to stop him. It was too much, too exposed. It went against my need to stay invisible. I shook my head. "I can't..."

My protest disappeared and my head fell backward as the lips and tongue that had been on my breast found my core. "Oh..." As if suddenly weak, my elbows gave out and I fell back on the soft pillows.

Tongue.

Teeth.

Lick.

Nip.

Suck.

Lifting my fist to my mouth, I bit down, trying unsuccessfully to stifle the sounds I was incapable of stopping. It didn't matter what I did or said—not that I was conscious of what that all entailed.

My hips bucked.

My fingers entwined in his blond hair.

My thighs tightened around his head.

He didn't stop until I was again in an uncontrolled free fall.

When I didn't think I could take any more, Patrick climbed up my body. His solid warmth hovered over me as he said, "I told you, I missed your taste. No one tastes like you. You're a fucking juicy apple to a starved soul."

He was such a good man.

I didn't deserve him. I never had.

For one night, I wanted to remember.

I reached up and cupped his cheeks, bringing his lips to mine, tasting my essence as we again became one. Slower at first, we moved in sync. It was like riding a bike—the one you loved as a kid that has been lost and was now found. In Patrick's arms with the scruff of his chin abrading my skin and his praises ringing in my ears, I was more.

More than a pussy to be fucked.

More than a woman repaying a debt with all that she had to give.

I was more.

It was an unusual sense of self-worth, one I had trouble comprehending. Not after everything.

Patrick stilled, lifting his face from my shoulder. "Push them away, Maddie. Push whatever thoughts are taking you away from me and this away from you. Look at me. Here. Now. This. That's all you're allowed to think about."

"How do you know?" I was a professional gambler, in poker and life. Not showing my emotions was key to my success. "How can you tell?"

"Because you're my wife. I know you. The way your body moves. It's carved in my memory." His thumb came to my cheek and wiped away a tear. "I don't want to make you cry."

My head shook. "You're not."

Reaching for my hips, Patrick rolled us until I was the one on top. "Fuck me, Maddie. After all, that's why you came to Chicago. Do it."

Leaning forward, my hands rested upon his broad shoulders as my long hair cascaded around us. I stared into his blue gaze. "That's not why I'm here."

"Those clouds? They can't get you if you're moving." He bucked his hips, moving his cock within me.

If only it was that easy to escape.

"You want me on top?" I asked.

"I want to watch my wife come as she rides me. Do it."

I took a deep breath. I'd done this before, but honestly, it had been a long time ago. For as long as I could remember, my place had been to take and accept, to willingly concede. There wasn't the opportunity for even the appearance of control. Yet that was what Patrick was offering.

Positioning my knees, I lifted myself, feeling the incredible sensation as his hard shaft teased my core. Slowly, I lowered myself. My lips parted as my painted nails clung tightly to his shoulders. I could do this. I could.

Lower, his fullness stretched me. Moving upward, I stretched my legs. Flexing them, I moved back down. Each change in position added to my confidence. Up and down. The sensations intensified and lessened depending upon my posture. It was pleasurable, empowering, and tiring.

My breathing grew shallower as my speed increased. Patrick's hands again came to my hips, helping and coordinating as the muscles in my thighs cried out in exhaustion.

"Come here."

His deep voice penetrated the sex-induced fog that had taken residence in my mind. I was so close to the edge. With pleasure dominating my thoughts, the clouds had passed. I stilled, trying to understand what he'd said. "Here? Where?" I asked.

His strong hands lifted me, pulling me off and forward.

"What?"

"You're almost there. I'm going to take over."

Oh my God.

My stomach twisted. He didn't want me to ride his cock but his face. "Patrick...I-I..."

He pulled each knee to beside his face as I reached for the top of the headboard.

I couldn't describe what happened next. There weren't words.

My teeth came down on the wooden headboard as I came, over and over, my insides clenching to a painful pitch as my knees squeezed his head and my essence flowed over his tongue. By the time it ended, I had nothing left.

Like a wilting flower, I collapsed onto the bed.

"Tomorrow, we talk."

It was the last thing I heard before I drifted away.

MADELINE

*P*ounding infiltrated my dreams.

Rapid.

Repeating.

Ripping away the veil of slumber.

Revealing reality.

"What?" I asked too softly to be heard.

"Madeline, open the damn door."

Fuck.

Mitchell's angry voice caused my eyes to open as I tried to make sense of my surroundings. I pushed to sit, my naked body moving on the soft sheets. As I readjusted myself in the darkened room, I groaned.

Damn, every muscle ached as my legs straightened. Even my breasts were tender under the weight of the covers. A grin came to my lips recalling Patrick's proclamation. 'Tomorrow when you walk, sit, or even fucking stand still, I want you to feel me, to know that I was where I belong. I want you to think about everything I did to you. Every way you came until you couldn't come again. Mrs. Kelly, I want you to admit that you belong with me.'

I didn't admit it, not verbally. I never would. I could admit, at least to myself, that as I moved, I was remembering him and what he'd done.

My head turned from side to side.

When we'd finally fallen asleep the night before, the drapes were open and the lights were still on. Now as I looked around, the room appeared, other than the tangled sheets around me, as if it had been prepared for sleep, drapes drawn and lights out.

There was another stark difference between when I fell asleep and now.

I ran my palm over the sheets. The bed beside me was cool and empty.

"Goddamn it, open the fucking door or I'm getting a key and someone from the hotel."

I didn't have time to think about Patrick's departure as Mitchell's warning reverberated through the room.

"No, wait," I called toward him as I forced my sore legs to move and free me from the sheets. "Mitchell, I'm here. Give me a damn minute."

After freeing myself from the tangle of sheets, I flung the covers over the bed. Next, I made my way to the window and threw back the curtain. The action brought light to the room, causing me to squint at the blue sky beyond the ice-encrusted window.

My foot touched something soft. Looking down, I smiled, finding my robe where it had been dropped near the window. As I bent to pick it up, something caught my eye.

Shit.

Opening the drapes did more than bring illumination. Set in a crystallized impression upon the glass were multiple handprints and possibly forehead prints confirming my memories of their creation. Shaking my head, I closed the curtain and reached for a lamp, twisting its switch. It definitely wasn't as revealing.

The window needed to be cleaned. It wouldn't take a genius to figure out how the handprints had happened on the window. Not that Mitchell was even close to a genius, but he was a man.

"Just a minute," I called again as I hurried around, picking up my discarded clothes, my dress that had at some point fallen from the bed and my panties. Stepping into the panties, I pulled them into place, wrapped the robe from the floor tighter around me, and secured the sash. Taking a deep breath, I made my way to the door.

Before opening it, I quickly peered around the room. As last night's reconnection had not been limited to the bed, the room was in a bit of disarray. Flipping the switch, I peered into the empty bathroom. A quick check of my reflection made me grin. My hair was a mess and most of my makeup was gone, and my lips were still pink. I lifted my fingers to them. Tender. Yes, bruised from kissing was a good way to be. After running my fingers through my hair, I returned to the entryway.

My quick search was the last mission to confirm that I was definitely alone.

While it gave me a twinge of sadness, with Mitchell outside, it was better.

Looking back at the door, I noticed the chain unhooked. That made sense since Patrick left sometime during the night.

"Madeline, now," Mitchell's growl came from behind the door.

Sliding the chain lock closed, I opened the door as far as possible. "What?" I asked, sounding as exasperated as I felt.

"It's after ten in the morning. The boss is livid and you're fucked."

I had been, but not as he was saying.

My neck straightened. "Why? The tournament doesn't continue until tonight."

Mitchell's gaze went to the chain and back to me. His words came from between gritted teeth. "Open the goddamned door. This isn't a public conversation."

Common sense told me not to allow an irritated man with anger issues into my room. However, when it came to Andros and therefore Mitchell, common sense didn't apply. Mitchell was here because of the boss, because of Andros, and I knew from experience, arguing wouldn't bode well. With a shake of my head, I closed the door and slid open the chain lock.

As soon as the knob turned on my side, Mitchell pushed the door open from his. I stepped out of the way in time for it to bounce off the interior wall.

Without a word, he stalked inside, scanning the room, walking near the windows and back, and eyeing the bed where despite my attempt, the covers were in all kinds of disarray. He pushed past me, gazing into the bathroom.

What was he thinking?

Did he know there was a man here last night?

His search only increased my already-rapid pulse. "What are you doing? Why are you in my room?"

"Where the fuck is your phone?"

"What? My phone?"

"I don't see it plugged in." He pointed to the charger on the nightstand. "Your GPS has gone silent and you haven't answered any calls."

Fuck. No wonder Andros is pissed.

Looking around, I tried to recall. I'd had my purse at the tournament. My phone was in my handbag. "Oh shit. I forgot to plug it in last night. It's in my purse." I hurried to the side of the bed where I'd left my handbag last night before Patrick's arrival. I was certain I'd laid it on the nightstand. I ran my hand over the glossy surface. "I swear it was here."

Tendons came to life in Mitchell's thick neck as he silently stared. "Where is your purse?"

"Um...Let me think," I muttered as my eyes hastily scanned the room.

My mind tried to recall what I'd done, but there was only one thought.

Patrick.

It wasn't only my phone that my purse contained.

Shit, I felt faint. Inside my purse was the chips receipt worth forty grand.

Did Patrick know that?

Had he watched at the club?

My stomach twisted with my knowledge.

The Patrick I knew, the younger version, was an expert pickpocket. He could lift a man's wallet, take out one bill or five and return it before the victim was the wiser. It was better than stealing the entire thing. Most of the time, the victims never realized they'd been targeted. Tourists were too focused on the sights. The loss of a twenty-dollar bill could be chalked up to forgetfulness. That wasn't all. We could go into a shop and I'd buy a candy bar, but when we walked out, he'd have crackers or cookies and a bottle of soda pop. With the shop owner's attention on me, he or she would never know what happened.

I didn't want to have the thoughts I was having, but I couldn't come up with an alternative.

Had Patrick moved on to bigger heists?

Was anything last night real?

"Your fucking phone," Mitchell repeated. "You didn't answer it last night or this morning, and now the GPS is dead. Find it now."

I stood and walked around the room, lifting the dress I'd thrown onto the sofa and hurrying into the bathroom. The counter was filled with cosmetics but no phone. I went back into the room, my hands beginning to tremble. "I-I...the ringer was off at the tournament. I guess I forgot to turn it back on."

"You forgot? You knew the boss would call."

I did. "I forgot."

With his lips thinning to a menacing sneer, Mitchell came closer. "I don't think he'll consider that an acceptable excuse. And I don't need to tell you that he's fucking pissed. When you tell him the purse is gone..." He didn't finish. He didn't need to.

I took a step back. "It's not gone. I-I just need to locate it."

Mitchell's eyes opened wide—he'd just connected the dots. "The fucking receipt?"

I swallowed. "The receipt is with my phone in the purse. I remember seeing it when we were in the taxi." I looked up at his dark eyes. "Remember? You said something about it."

Shaking his head, he let out a long exhale. "Fuck, you have really screwed up."

"No. No." My volume rose as I began pacing. Trembling was no longer isolated to my hands. My body was ready to go into full-blown tremors. "Listen. Just stop. It has to be here." I prayed it was. "I fell asleep. It was a late—" There were no alternatives I could conjure. Andros was already angry that I'd ignored his calls and Mitchell's knocks. That would be nothing compared to his wrath at losing the receipt worth forty grand and not making the cut.

He would lose his shit—or worse.

"Please, Mitchell," I said, "give me time." I began tossing the pillows, praying for what I believed wasn't present.

Shit.

I'd let down my guard.

With a sigh, I turned and stared into Mitchell's gaze, fighting the tears pooling in my eyes.

I wasn't a crier. I wasn't a lot of things, or at least, I'd learned not to be.

The consequences of last night would be far greater than sore muscles.

Patrick accused me of coming to town to fuck with him. In reality, he'd tracked me down to do the same.

Literally and now figuratively.

'I want to kill you or fuck you.'

My knees gave way at the building nausea as I sank to the edge of the bed. It seemed he'd done both. Because losing Andros's money would be my death.

A tear escaped my lower lid and tracked down my cheek.

With my head tilted forward, I saw Mitchell's shoes as he neared. Swallowing the tears, I looked up and lifted my hand, palm forward. "Please, Mitchell, stop. I was asleep." I looked down at the robe. "I mean look at me. You woke me. I was exhausted last night. I told you that. I'm disoriented. The purse is here. I had it in the cab and at the front counter last night, remember?"

He nodded.

"Okay. Just give me a damn minute. I'll find it, and I'll be ready for tonight's tournament."

Indecision showed in his eyes when he reached in his pocket, pulling out his phone. Without a word, he placed a call.

I wrapped my arms around my midsection, knowing who would be on the other end. Bile continued to churn in my stomach, reminding me that I'd never called for room service.

That's what I needed, food.

Right, because food would save me from Andros.

"Yes, sir," Mitchell said into his phone as he continued to gaze my direction. "She's here. It looks like she's been asleep." Pause. "No, I don't think so." His shoulders shrugged. "I don't know." He looked at me. "You leave the room since I left you here?"

My head shook. It was one question I could answer honestly. "No. I didn't."

"Yes, sir." Mitchell handed his phone my direction with a warning gaze. "He wants to talk to you."

PATRICK

*T*hree sets of eyes turned my direction as the metal door slid open and I entered two.

Two was how we referred to the floor of our compound high in Chicago's skyline that contained the headquarters for the Sparrow outfit. In reality, it was the ninety-fourth story of one of Chicago's tallest buildings, the floor that was only accessible to the elite in the organization. It was where the leaders of the outfit did what we did, what we do now, run Chicago.

Underground and aboveground.

Nothing happened without our approval.

On this floor with our wealth of technology we were capable of monitoring the streets of our city in a way outfits of the past never imagined. That didn't mean we didn't have eyes and ears on the ground, we did. The technology was our way of confirming that whatever the eyes and ears told us was accurate.

One set of eyes looking my way belonged to the kingpin, the boss of Chicago's underworld, a Fortune 500 CEO, and one of my closest friends, Sterling Sparrow. The other two sets belonged to the other two men, also my close friends that Sparrow and I had the honor of serving our country with before focusing our talents on the 234 square miles known as Chicago: Reid Murray and Mason Pierce.

Taking a deep breath, I ran my hand over my damp, freshly showered hair.

"Late night?" Sparrow asked.

"Later than I planned," I replied.

I'd stayed with Maddie until late into the night, actually early in the morning. Leaving her took more willpower than I feared I could muster. She was so fucking beautiful lying there, her long hair mussed, makeup smeared or worn away, her lips bruised and swollen, and the best part: her soft, warm, naked body curled against me like it had been long ago in a ratty old sleeping bag. Damn, even thinking about it made my dick twitch.

It had been nearing four this morning when I made it back here and to my apartment one story above us. For all I knew, some of these men may have been up and working right where we now were. However, appearing in the middle of the night disheveled and fresh from the best sex of my life didn't seem like the wise choice—not if I didn't want a thousand questions or to reveal the secret I didn't realize I had withheld over the years until I saw Madeline.

After a quick shower, I collapsed into bed only to wake about thirty minutes ago to an hour-old text from Reid asking why I wasn't here. Instead of answering, I showered again, grabbed a mug of hot coffee, and made my way to two, our headquarters.

Taking a drink of steaming coffee, I looked up at the screen overhead, the focus of everyone's attention. "Did I miss something?"

"You were there. We're waiting for you to fill us in," Mason said.

Sitting in the empty chair, I stared upward. What was before us appeared to be an aerial view, similar to Google maps, but with real-time accuracy. Reid had figured out how to tap into not only street cameras and private security feeds, but also satellite feeds. What made that even more impressive, not that it wasn't, was that with Mason's help, they'd discovered how to control the focus, zooming in and out, again in real time. I wasn't bad at the whole technology thing and neither was Sparrow. However, neither of us boasted of knowing more than our resident technology geeks.

Lack of sleep wasn't unusual in our world. When there were fires—literal and metaphoric—needing our attention, we could go days with only small catnaps. The difference for me was that last night wasn't a usual fire. It was a different kind of fire, one simmering in my soul. Everything that happened last night had my mind spinning and my body on overdrive.

I shook my head. "The snow from a few days ago is still covering rooftops. Help a man out. What am I seeing?"

"Where were you last night, Patrick?" Sparrow asked.

While I could have inferred more from his question, his tone didn't suggest an issue.

"Club Regal," I replied. "The first round of their big poker tournament was last night. It started with forty-two players, each one paying a hefty entrance fee. Now it's down to thirty." It was as I answered, I realized that was what we were seeing, the rooftops of Club Regal as well as neighboring buildings.

"The rumors are flying at all levels of the city," Reid said. "Tell us if it's true."

Rumors?

I hadn't expected that.

Who saw me and Madeline talking?

Was I spotted going into her hotel room or leaving?

Lifting my coffee, I stood, taking a few steps as I determined the best strategy for my confession, for telling my three best friends that I'd left a small yet significant part out of my biography. It wasn't something I was prepared to admit. Nevertheless, they deserved to know. The sentences formed in my head. *Oh, by the way, when I was eighteen, before I met all of you, I married this girl. A few months later she disappeared. Word on the street was that she died, the casualty of random violence. It happens even today. When I found no clues, I gave up. I joined the army to get away from the memories. But, hey, don't worry. Last night I saw her again. And since we never divorced, she's still my wife.*

Then Reid's deep voice penetrated my fog.

"...said he bought in. He left town after his dad and McFadden went down. Why would he come back?"

I let out a long breath.

They weren't talking about Maddie. The rumors they'd mentioned were about Antonio Hillman, a man with close connections to the now-defunct McFadden outfit, the outfit that had co-ruled Chicago since before any of us were born, the one whose leader was now serving time for unimaginable crimes against children.

I focused on what I'd heard. "At the end of the night," I said, "before announcing the placements for round two, the club made the announcement about Hillman."

"And you didn't think it was significant?" Mason asked.

My neck straightened. "I did. It was. It is." I took a breath. "Antonio wasn't there. I checked the entire club. I didn't see anyone who was previously in his or his father's entourage. According to the announcement, the younger Hillman is supposed to arrive to Club Regal tonight."

"He's a cocky son of a bitch," Reid said.

Sparrow stood. "I don't like it. The move is fucking brazen. The money-laundering son of McFadden's imprisoned consigliere, who hasn't been seen around here since his father's trial, comes back to Chicago and not under the radar. He comes back paying seventy-five grand to buy into a poker tournament. Why?"

"He wasn't convicted of the money laundering," Reid said.

"Because he was never charged," I added. "The feds concentrated on Rubio and Wendell."

"Which, as we've been saying, leaves other players in the McFadden outfit we haven't gotten to yet, ones who disappeared, like Antonio." Sparrow inhaled and lifted both hands to the top of his head. His biceps flexed beneath the sleeves of his gray t-shirt like they did when he was concentrating. "There's something else happening." Sparrow turned to me. "Tell us everything about Club Regal last night. Everything. I'm fucking ecstatic that we had a man on the scene. One of the best." He reached for a chair, spun it around, and straddled the back. "Was there anything that felt unusual? Anything or anyone who stood out—caught your attention?"

Shit.

Yes, but I wasn't ready to say, not until I knew more.

I began recounting my honest memories of the night, the

patrons, security, and the tournament itself. During those recollections, I conveniently excluded mentioning Madeline; however, I did mention the high roller Marion Elliott. There had been a constant buzz of whispers at his presence. I'd done some research and he deserved the hype. He had one of the longest lists of tournament wins and therefore, one of the highest lifetime earnings. His age was an obvious contributing factor.

"I saw him," I said, "and watched him play. He deserves his reputation, but he's also old."

Reid was typing on another keyboard. On a different screen, Marion Elliott's picture appeared. "This him?"

"Yeah," I replied, "but that picture is old or photoshopped. Last night, he looked ten years older, at least."

"It says here," Reid began to read, "Marion Elliott, born in Houston, Texas." He nodded as he continued reading. "Well, according to this he's thirty years older than us."

Of course, we didn't all have the same birth date. However, all joining the army at eighteen and meeting in basic training, we were close in age. The four of us exchanged looks as we contemplated Reid's finding.

"How old is McFadden now?" I asked.

"Early seventies," Sparrow said. "My father would be one year older." He took a deep breath. "I don't know. There's no known connection to this Elliott and McFadden's outfit."

"None has come up so far," Mason said.

"Yeah, it doesn't mean it didn't exist," I said. "And we know there's a connection between Hillman and McFadden."

"Why here? Why now?" Reid asked.

"Because since we've squashed McFadden, every two-bit hustler thinks Chicago is ripe for the picking," Sparrow said with more than a bit of exasperation to his tone. "It's fucking exhausting."

"You proved them all wrong when you took over the Sparrow outfit and then when you squashed McFadden," I said. "You'll continue to prove them wrong now. I think it has to do with McFadden himself. He was fucking diversified and his trial received a lot of press. Now he's appealing the trafficking charges and it's all over the news media outlets. It's like an advertisement to people near and far: come to Chicago and take Rubio McFadden's place at the top of the city. These assholes don't know you or what Sparrow is capable of achieving. Fuck, what we have achieved."

I wasn't kissing up because I'd lost focus last night. I believed every damn word I was saying.

"They don't know the Sparrow outfit," Sparrow replied. "We need to be on this one hundred percent. I don't like what I'm feeling. I can't fucking put my finger on it, but damn, it's—"

"Gut," Mason said. "I trust any one of our guts more than all the fucking technology in this room." Mason turned to me. "How did Elliott respond when the announcement was made about Hillman's buy-in?"

Elliott wasn't who had my attention.

"The whole room was pissed," I said. "Gasps and murmurs and shit. I was surprised Club Regal would allow it on the second day. It seemed shitty to me."

"Did he seem surprised?" Mason asked.

I shook my head. "One of the best poker players in the world doesn't show emotion."

While my friends nodded, my mind went to one poker player who finally did. When I arrived at her hotel room, I hadn't been sure that we could be honest with one another, Madeline and I. But we were, at least physically we were—raw, primal, and fucking real.

Sparrow's pacing came to a stop. He turned a 180 and looked my way. His brown eyes were open wide. "What did you just say?"

"Not showing emotion?" Fuck, I was having trouble keeping up.

"No," Mason said, his eyes widening too. "About Club Regal."

Sparrow nodded. "Yes, exactly. It might be shitty, but the club allowed Hillman's buy-in."

As Reid and I exchanged looks, for a moment I was pleased to not be the only person not following this train of thought.

Sparrow's grin grew. "We all know which one of us is the best chess player." His dark gaze went to Mason who shook his head.

The two of them had been arguing their supremacy for as long as I could remember.

"I'd put my money on Patrick at a poker table," Sparrow went on. "Cards are nothing more than math and memory. Fucking no one in this room is better at either than you." He was looking directly at me.

By the time he finished speaking, my blood had cooled until it settled near my feet. I rarely felt light-headed, but now I did. I could cut a man's throat and watch him bleed out. This was different. I reached for the chair. "You want me to buy in to Club Regal's tournament? Now? And play tonight?"

"Fuck yes," Sparrow replied. "Hillman got in for seventy-five. Make a phone call, or better yet, a visit. There's no way the club will deny a request from Sparrow. Not if they want to stay in business. Hillman has been quiet for a while now, but damn, I'd guess his buy-in was paid for by dirty McFadden money. That fucking old man may be rotting in prison for the rest of his life, but he's not going to lie down and let me rule. His hatred is too strong. He wants revenge. And that could include Araneae. We aren't allowing it. This needs to end."

Araneae was his wife. Is his wife.

"They ranked Hillman at the bottom of tonight's play, number thirty," I said.

Sparrow nodded. "Seventy-five grand got him the bottom of the barrel. Find out what a hundred Gs and a twenty-five percent reduction in this tournament's taxes will do."

My eyes opened wide. That's a crazy amount of money. "And you expect me to stay in this tournament and to make it to tomorrow?"

The grin growing across Sparrow's face reached his eyes. "No, I don't expect that."

I exhaled.

"I expect you to win the whole fucking thing."

MADELINE

*W*illing my hand not to shake, I reached out for Mitchell's phone. One breath in and one breath out. I closed my eyes, imagining the face of the man on the other end of the call. The image wasn't comforting. Andros was the leader of the Ivanov bratva for a reason. He was nearly ten years my senior, tall and broad, with a commanding voice that could intimidate the toughest capos. He also had a stare that could send shivers down your spine. A cold, dead stare like that of a shark. Andros sensed prey the same way the shark smelled blood. It was an uncanny ability that no doubt aided in his position.

I'd stood dutifully nearby as he'd ordered horrendous crimes against men and women, knowing he took a perverse pleasure in the knowledge of their suffering. I'd been his release for pleasure and anger. I'd watched as he rejoiced in victories and raged over defeats. No matter the circumstance, nothing brought life to his dark eyes.

With one last deep breath, I put the phone to my ear. "Hello, Andros."

For a moment, I thought maybe I'd waited too long to speak and that the line had gone dead.

For only a moment.

"My dear, I've been worried."

To the untrained ear, the kingpin of Detroit's underground may sound gentlemanly or even debonair. That same person could misconstrue his liquid-silk baritone timbre as sincerity and his words as concern.

I wasn't untrained.

Years of servitude had taught me hard lessons.

Andros Ivanov was not gentlemanly, debonair, sincere, or concerned.

Yes, he could imitate those qualities.

If I were a man in his bratva who had ignored his calls—I hoped he didn't know about the chip receipt—my greeting no doubt would have been harsher. If we were together in the same room, I was most certain it would be also.

I said a small prayer of thanksgiving that neither of those circumstances was different.

"I'm sorry," I said, "I didn't mean to worry you. I hope you know that. This wasn't intentional."

"Hope. It's such an interesting choice of word—to hope is to feel expectation. You see, my dear, that was what I had last night upon hearing from Mitchell that you had returned safely to your room, had recovered most of my losses, and secured a seat at tonight's tables. I had hope. My hope was to discuss it with you personally."

"All of those things happened. And when I returned to the

room, I was more exhausted than I realized. The ringer was off at the tournament, and I forgot to turn it on. I wasn't avoiding your call. I fell sound asleep."

"How many?" he asked.

"How many...what?"

"Tell me how many times I called and how many times you didn't answer."

My head shook as my eyes again scanned the room. Maybe if I opened the curtains I could see the room better and find my purse, but if I opened the curtains... My gaze went to Mitchell.

Did he know the answer to Andros's question?

It didn't matter. Mitchell wasn't here to be my savior.

"That's the problem, Andros," I replied. "With everything last night, I'm having trouble this morning locating my phone. Once I do I promise I'll plug it in. I won't leave here until it's fully charged. Mitchell can verify that."

"Remember the number. It will be significant in the future."

Such as a stone dropping in my stomach, my experience told me that whatever his plan, it wouldn't be good. My hope was winning. Money was Andros's greatest distraction.

"Mitchell told me about the buy-in," he said. "Highly unusual."

"It is," I agreed, thankful he'd moved on to another topic. "I'd never heard of it happening until now. The man's name..." I couldn't recall. "...I don't remember." My mind had been on two things: securing my spot and Patrick. "I'm sorry."

"Hillman. Antonio Hillman."

"Yes."

"What else haven't you told me?"

My eyes momentarily closed. There was much I hadn't told

him, wouldn't tell him. Seeing Patrick was my secret just like being married to him was. After the tournament, Mitchell and I would travel back to Detroit and life would resume. This reconnection with Patrick wouldn't and couldn't change that. There was no need to make it into anything more than it was. And if I mentioned his visit last night, I would open myself up for an interrogation about the purse.

"Madeline, dear. Do you truly believe hesitation is in your best interest?"

"I was trying to recall what I haven't said. I'm still fuzzy from Mitchell's abrupt wake-up."

"Go on."

Standing, I walked over to the desk. With the phone secured between my ear and shoulder, I wrote a note as I spoke. "I recognized a few of the tournament players. I don't recognize the name of the man who bought in."

I pushed the note toward Mitchell.

Does he know about my missing handbag?

Mitchell shook his head.

"Should I recognize it?" I asked, continuing my conversation with Andros as I wrote again.

I pushed the note back Mitchell's way.

Please give me time. Please, I can make this right.

. . .

"I don't know why you would," Andros said. "Hillman hasn't been around until lately and you know I don't allow anyone near you unless they have my complete trust."

"So you know him?" I asked, trying to keep the conversation away from my phone or purse and definitely away from admitting I'd allowed someone into my room, and I'd been swindled out of $40,000. "And you don't trust him?"

"I didn't say that. Don't make assumptions where I'm concerned. I would think you would have learned that."

Asshole. Yes, I've learned.

My gaze went to Mitchell and I tilted my head in a silent plea.

"I'm not assuming," I replied to Andros. "I'm wondering, should I be concerned about his play? Do you think he'll try something dishonest?" I covered the microphone of the phone. "Please?" I whispered to Mitchell.

"You owe me," Mitchell growled. "And you don't have long. I'll deny knowing."

My head was nodding. I wasn't sure what I'd owe. Whatever it was, it would be worth it to save me a bit of Andros's wrath.

"Dishonest," Andros repeated. "I'm most certain of it, as certain as I am of your ability to win no matter what. I'm still waiting for you to tell me what you haven't. Hurry now. I'm a busy man."

At least I knew it wasn't about the purse. That left Patrick and I... "I'm sorry. What haven't I told you?"

"A man touched what is mine and you don't think I should know?"

"Touched?" My pulse began to race as my knees gave way. With trembling resuming, I again landed on the edge of the bed.

"Madeline." His tone deepened as he issued his command. "Stay away from Marion Elliott."

Marion Elliott.

I exhaled with relief.

"His attention isn't simply because you're beautiful," Andros went on. "He knows of your reputation and ability. He wants to charm you into being unnerved."

"I promise, I can handle myself with Marion Elliott. I'm not charmed. If I had been, our encounter would have been more memorable. He simply asked me to join him for a drink, and I declined."

"He kissed you."

My neck straightened at his continuing change in tone. He may be upset I didn't answer his calls, but he was more upset about Marion Elliott's pleasantries.

"My hand," I said softly. "He kissed my hand."

"I don't share what is mine unless it's to my benefit."

I wasn't his.

I wasn't his *dear* or his property to be shared.

My servitude was a debt I could never repay. That didn't mean I was property to be claimed.

It was the mantra I told myself when the lines in reality began to blur.

I took a breath. "Andros, I just woke. You're busy. I will have my phone charged soon, and I will see the number of times you've called. Tonight, after the tournament, I will turn on the ringer and personally tell you that I have advanced to tomorrow's afternoon round, that I'm part of the top eighteen, and that I stayed clear of Marion Elliott. May I go now?"

"Return the phone to Mitchell. I expect to see the location of your phone soon."

"Goodbye," I said, handing the phone to Mitchell. As I did, my lips mouthed my silent plea.

"Boss," he said into the phone. "Yes, I did. Let me step into the hallway."

As soon as the door closed and latched, I let out an exaggerated breath and flopped onto the bed. Just because I'd avoided telling Andros the truth about my purse and its missing status didn't negate the fact it was gone.

Staring up at the ceiling, I lifted my hands to my temples and pushed in an effort to stop the recent throbbing.

The action wouldn't locate my purse, the receipt, or the phone, but it helped me think. Something else that would help was breakfast. With Patrick's visit, I had never called for dinner.

Making myself move, my first destination was a visit to the bathroom. After taking care of business, I splashed water onto my cheeks, removing the remnants of last night's makeup. As I did, I tested my cheek, finding it no longer tender and the color nearly normal. My neck too was bruise free.

There were other parts of my body that were tender. The thoughts of those aches brought a smile to my lips. Yes, Patrick, I remember you. And just as quickly the thoughts of elation faded.

Damn him.

Back out in the room, I called for room service. Once my breakfast was ordered, I returned to the window. Opening the drapes, I peered out at the city below, noticing how the morning sunlight had warmed the pane. The ice crystals from before were gone, making the evidence of last night's activities less obvious. If I hadn't seen them before, they could be easily missed.

My head tilted as I tried to find them.

This time my sentiment came in an audible form as I called out to the room, "Damn you, Patrick. How could you?"

I spun back toward the bed, wondering what additional evidence of our night could be found. Throwing back the blankets, I recalled our night. I couldn't remember the last time I'd fallen asleep in a man's arms.

"Damn you," I again proclaimed aloud. "Damn you for whatever game you think you're playing. Damn you for souring the memory of the one man I'd trusted."

I wasn't sure how I would do it, but I needed to find or contact him, and it had to be soon.

Would losing the receipt exclude me from the tournament?

I wasn't certain. I'd never had this issue before.

That couldn't happen.

MADELINE

"*I* don't know what else to do," I said to Mitchell. "Nothing in my purse is as valuable as the receipt. Everything else can be replaced."

His head shook as we rode side by side in the back seat of another taxi on our way to Club Regal. "You better pray they have a copy."

I was.

I was praying with a vigor I hadn't in years.

"This can't be the first time something like this has happened." It was the first time it happened to me. My gaze went out the window to the street and sidewalk. Despite the cooler temperatures, people in heavy coats, hats, gloves, and boots, were scurrying along. Missions didn't wait for weather. With their heads down to the wind, they trudged on. It reminded me of the people in Detroit. These people were hardy when it came to cold weather.

"You showed your ID at the desk," Mitchell said.

"I know."

"You said you didn't leave the room."

"I didn't."

His tone lowered. "Listen, I didn't tell Andros because my ass is on the line too, but so help me God, I won't go down for this. You're lying about something. There's no way your whole purse disappeared, magically vanished during the night." He paused for a moment like he was reviewing the evening. "I know you had it when we got to your room. You opened the door. I suppose you will need a third key."

"I will," I said, my mind swirling with more thoughts. My temples continued to throb and the breakfast I'd eaten about an hour ago was doing cartwheels in my stomach. The receipt was the most important item, but now my mind was on other things.

My phone could reveal to Patrick the world of the Ivanov bratva. I didn't want to worry about him, not after he did this to me. Nevertheless, one call to the wrong person could enter Patrick into a world he didn't know existed. "I know it doesn't make sense."

"You searched again?" he asked.

"I did."

I hadn't. My gut told me I'd been robbed. My body obviously led me astray, but my gut was rarely wrong.

"Did you tip the person who delivered you dinner?" he asked.

His questions wouldn't stop. I liked him better when he was silent. "I didn't eat dinner."

Mitchell's neck straightened.

"I fell asleep," I explained again, sticking to my story. "I didn't eat until this morning, and I tipped on the receipt, not in cash." I lay my head back on the seat and closed my eyes, hoping

Mitchell would take the hint and let this conversation rest. There was nothing we were going to solve in this taxi.

The cab came to a stop outside Club Regal. After Mitchell paid the fare and we exited the car, I buried my gloved hands deep into the pockets of my coat and stared up at the building. The limestone architecture was ornate and the red awning rich. Even if one didn't know this was a private club, it would be obvious that the clients within had a great deal of money.

The doorman must have recognized us from last night as he simply nodded and opened the heavy door. Unlike last night when we'd arrived after nightfall, now entering from the sunny street made the club—the paneling and carpeting—seem ominously darker than before.

It was like walking into a well-furnished cave, isolated from the world.

"Ms. Miller," a woman called as she came my way. She was older with short blonde hair and a regal air. Her black dress and pumps were simple yet elegant as was her single string of pearls. Though we hadn't previously met, I was certain she worked for the club.

"Yes."

Nodding to Mitchell, she offered her hand to me. "Hello, I'm Veronica. I work here, specifically with events such as your tournament. I didn't get a chance to talk to you last night and introduce myself. I wanted to tell you that we here at Club Regal were pleased you agreed to join us for this tournament." Her voice lowered. "And if I can confess, I'm rooting for you. We've never crowned a female champion."

I smiled. "Thank you. I would be honored to be the first."

"However," she said, looking at her wristwatch. "You are early for tonight's activities."

"I am. I was wondering if we might have a word in private."

"Yes, of course. My office is back this way." She gestured away from the restaurant, bar, and front door. "We can speak there. I hope there's not a problem."

I turned to Mitchell. "I'll find you when we're done."

His Adam's apple bobbed. "Ma'am, under the circumstances—"

"Thank you, Mitchell," I interrupted dismissively, then turned and began walking the direction Veronica led.

I didn't get far when his large hand grasped my upper arm. Leaning in close, he whispered, "You better do what you discussed. Be clear, if you fuck with me, I'm not going down alone."

Veronica stopped and turned our way. "Is everything all right?"

My gaze went from Mitchell's beady stare to his hand still on my arm. My voice was hushed. "I told you what would happen if you touched me again."

Slowly his grasp released. "Ms. Miller."

I took a deep breath and smiled toward Veronica. "Everything is fine. My associate will wait out here."

"The Bar Regal is open," she said. "You're welcome to wait in there."

"Thank you, ma'am."

The splendor of the club disappeared as we entered a locked hallway with doors lining each side. "This is..."

Sterile.

Plain.

Quite the contrast.

I wasn't certain how to describe it.

"This is our secure area, behind the scenes," she replied. "I hope it won't ruin the facade."

"No, I like it. It feels less pretentious."

With a keycard from her pocket, Veronica opened the door to what I assumed was her office. Flipping a switch, she gestured me into her space. The room was not large, but it was cozier than I expected. A large L-shaped desk faced two walls in the corner. There was a leather sofa along another wall, bookcases, and a small table and two chairs. There was a separate door slightly ajar. At first glance, I assumed it was her private bathroom.

"May I take your coat, Ms. Miller?"

"Madeline, please."

"Madeline."

Removing my gloves, I placed them in my coat pockets and unfastened the large buttons. My boots were high heeled and my hair was pulled back in a low ponytail. Beneath the coat, I was wearing casual slacks with a sweater. My makeup was minimal. I wasn't dressed for the tournament.

With a quick scan of my appearance, she asked, "Are you planning to stay until tonight?"

"No. May I?" I gestured to the table.

I liked that she didn't have the chairs across from her desk. This woman was confident enough in her position to forgo having the furniture arranged for a power play.

"Yes, of course," she said. After hanging my coat on a hall tree, she sat across the table. "Now, what brought you here this afternoon?"

"Veronica, I came today in person because I have a highly unusual situation."

With a scoff, she shook her head. "When it comes to this particular tournament, I'm no longer shocked. Everything about it has been unusual, and it seems to be getting more irregular by the minute."

Folding my hands on my lap, I leaned back. If this woman was going to confide in me about anything, it bettered my chances of remaining in the tournament. "You don't say? What's odd?"

"I really shouldn't mention it."

"I don't think it's cheating to understand the tournament. And..." I brightened my smile. "...you did say you're rooting for me."

Her lips thinned as lines of contemplation showed on her forehead. "The buy-in. I wasn't consulted. Not that it's my decision, it's not. It's Mr. Beckman's. However, it's highly unusual just the same and I voiced that opinion. I told Mr. Beckman that it set a precedent. He assured me that it would be all right. One time and done." She exhaled again as her lips formed a straight line.

"Are you saying that you were right? Someone else wants to buy in?"

"Highly unusual."

My mind was churning. "I suppose if someone didn't make the cut, they would perhaps give that a chance."

"Oh goodness," she said, "you're right. That wasn't what happened, but this is a mess. I think it needs to be stated in no uncertain terms that no more buy-ins are possible after tonight's round. Mr. Beckman disagrees. He said to do that would shine the spotlight on the two gentlemen."

I sat taller. "Two?"

"Well, I suppose you'll find out tonight anyway. You heard the announcement about Mr. Hillman."

I nodded.

"The other buy-in is a member of the club. If we allowed Mr. Hillman who is no longer a member, it was impossible to refuse Mr. Kelly."

My eyes blinked as I tried to process. "Excuse me? Mr. Kelly?" Surely it wasn't my Mr. Kelly. He wouldn't do that, enter a tournament where I was playing, where I needed to win.

"Patrick Kelly," Veronica said. "You wouldn't know him."

I shrugged, afraid to speak and reveal that I did know him. He's the reason I'm here, the reason my purse is missing. He stole my purse and now he'd stolen a player's spot.

Could he attempt to use my chips?

"What will that do to the lineup? Will someone arrive who is expecting to play only to learn he won't?" I hadn't been paying attention to all the placements, and then I recalled that Antonio Hillman was announced as number thirty. "Will this Mr. Kelly's addition remove Mr. Hillman from play?"

"It's a mess. We can't do that. We accepted his buy-in."

I sat taller. "And you accepted each player's entry fee."

"I know. I know. Ever since Mr. Kelly's visit with Mr. Beckman, I've been hoping someone would willingly drop out. I know that isn't right, but it would make things go smoother."

"He came in here...in person? When?" The rest of her statement registered. "Drop out?"

"Yes, it wasn't long ago. I believe he left just before your arrival."

My skin warmed.

Fuck.

If I tell her that I don't have my chip receipt, she could say I was disqualified. That would help her situation and open a spot for Patrick.

There was no way I could let that happen.

She waved her hand. "I apologize. You didn't come here to hear me complain." Her expression morphed into one of alarm. "Please forget what I said. It was wrong of me, an old lady's musings. I would never mean to insinuate that Club Regal would deny Mr. Kelly. I wouldn't want that to get out. It's not what I meant." Her words came faster. "I am simply exasperated at the whole precedent. I hope you understand."

Why was she suddenly nervous?

There was no way for her to know that I have had any association with Mr. Kelly.

"Ms... I mean Madeline," she said, leaning forward, "forget we had this talk. Let's regroup. Now, what was it you wanted to speak to me about?"

"I was just wondering if the club has record of our earnings thus far. I was curious if you retained that information or only we have our own receipts."

"The chips were counted, collected, and tagged accordingly. Despite all that has occurred, when you enter the hall tonight your receipt is merely your entry ticket. The dealers will confirm that your receipt matches their records and after the players are randomly assigned to the individual tables, you will be given your chips, the same ones you had last night. You know how superstitious gamblers are? We try to account for all circumstances."

"And if someone misplaced their receipt?"

"Madeline, this is far from your first go-round. You know that would put the club in a difficult spot."

I smiled. "It seems that is where the club is at this moment with Mr. Hillman and now Mr. Kelly."

"I hope you're not saying that your receipt is missing."

"If I were saying that, I would hope that Club Regal would be as accommodating to me as it has been to Mr. Hillman and Mr. Kelly. After all, we want a female to win, and I would hate for your displeasure regarding the recent situations to be repeated."

No, I wasn't above using her confession as leverage.

"Very well," Veronica said as she stood. "If you will join your associate in the bar for a few minutes, I can see what can be done."

My head tilted as I smiled. "I so appreciate your assistance. Thank you."

PATRICK

*A*fter securing my buy-in to the tournament, as I was leaving Club Regal, I peered into the mostly empty bar. I had places to go and work that needed tending, not to mention a tournament to play later tonight, yet at the sight of the man who had been with Madeline, I was drawn into Bar Regal. Apparently, last night, after a bit of questioning, the staff member I'd asked to delay this gentleman allowed his reentry to the second floor and the tournament. I hadn't had time to follow up other than to learn his name: Mitchell Leonardo.

I would learn more. Now I had the opportunity to do it in person.

Standing tall and squaring my shoulders, I stepped across the threshold. The interior was upscale. Bar Regal was subdivided into different rooms. The first one contained the shiny long bar surrounded by barstools. With one wall of tall windows, the afternoon sun shone upon the few tables near the bar, spotlighting the mirror and rows of high-end liquor bottles.

Most of the stools were unoccupied. The farther rooms had other tables as well as casual seating arrangements made up of plush sofas, chairs, and large round ottoman coffee tables. In the center of all the rooms was a grand piano, where live music was performed Thursday through Saturday nights.

The nearly barren state of the rooms wouldn't last. Daytime wasn't Club Regal's main hours of operation. Members who worked nearby the club often patronized the restaurant at lunchtime. However, Bar Regal picked up in pace later in the day. This may not have been how it was decades ago. I for one was happy that the two-martini lunch was no longer in vogue.

The reason I'd come inside—the man who had caught my attention—was sitting at the bar with his back to me as I entered. With his head down staring at his phone, he appeared to be nursing either straight vodka or a clear soda pop. As I neared, the bubbles moving up the inside of the glass revealed that whatever was inside was carbonated, ruling out vodka.

Settling on a nearby barstool, I scanned Mr. Leonardo's face in the large mirror over the bar. From his complexion, I would venture to guess he was in his upper forties to low fifties, had seen his share of the outdoors and had the weathered skin to prove it. While I wouldn't categorize him as overweight, even in his suit, I could tell that he had a few more pounds around the middle than I. His attire was above standard for this club. While his suit wasn't custom, it wasn't off the rack from some big box store either.

Whoever Mitchell Leonardo was, he had access to finances.

The bartender came toward me with a smile. "Mr. Kelly, what can I get you?"

While she was wearing a nametag, I didn't need to read it.

Tina had been working at Club Regal for at least five years. Private clubs appreciated employees who understood the nuances of the job. It wasn't like it was put in writing what to say and what not to say, but it was more than implied. When that valuable employee was found, he or she was paid well to stay in the position.

"Tina, I'd like water."

"On the rocks?" she asked with a grin.

"Yes, that would be good."

Mr. Leonardo lifted his chin as he watched Tina walk away. "She's a looker."

His observation left me unsettled, but if it was an opening for conversation, I'd take it. "Hmm."

The reality was that Tina wasn't my type.

Thoughts of Madeline infiltrated my thinking.

For someone I'd tried for years to remove from my thoughts —tried to forget—after only one night, less than twenty-four hours, I was suddenly consumed, addicted. Her beauty, soft skin, sweet aroma, and the melody of her voice ricocheted through my thoughts since seeing her at the poker table last night. Now, since being with her, it was difficult to concentrate on anything else.

However, my job required it.

I focused on the man to my left, careful not to let on that I knew much about him. "I think I saw you last night." We both maintained the unspoken etiquette of staring straight ahead, our only visual contact being within the mirror's reflection. "Are you new to Chicago?" I asked.

While knowing Mr. Leonardo was somehow associated with Madeline spurred my decision to enter the bar, my gut told me there was more to him. Something felt off. My allegiance to Sparrow wouldn't allow me to walk away.

"Passing through," he said.

"I believe you were watching the tournament last night. Are you a card player?"

"Nah. My passion is the ponies."

"Cards are easier to predict," I said. "Too many variables with horse racing."

The big man shrugged as he lifted his glass. "Not if you do your homework."

"Here you go," Tina said with a smile as she placed the glass of water before me. "May I get you anything else?"

"No, thank you. I need to be going soon." I returned to talking to the man. "If you're not a player, what brings you to the tournament?"

"This and that. I'm pulling for one of the players."

"A friend?" I asked.

"Yeah."

The way Madeline spoke to him in the hallway last evening, I wouldn't have categorized them as friends.

"So that's all you're doing is attending the tournament and then you will be gone?" I pushed.

Leonardo turned my way. "Excuse me. What's it to you?" His eyes had darkened circles beneath, giving him the appearance of being tired or distressed.

"As a member of this club, I like to keep track of who comes and goes. As a resident of this city, I do the same. It's part of what I do. As long as you're only here for the tournament, we should be good."

"This chat is over." His face tilted upward as his gaze went to the doorway. "My *friend* is here. I believe we'll be going."

When I turned to follow his gaze, my breath caught in my chest.

Our eyes locked.

I'd heard about tunnel vision before and seen it portrayed in movies. The fringes became fuzzy and blurred and all that could be seen was the one person in the center. I'd heard of it. I'd never before recalled experiencing it, not until this moment.

A goddess wrapped in a long wool coat, Madeline was stunning.

There was no doubt that she was the most beautiful woman I'd ever seen. She had been nearly twenty years ago, and she was more so today. Pink filled her cheeks as her stance straightened. Pulling her gaze away from me she focused on Leonardo.

The loss of her stare felt like the jolt of a freezing shower, cooling my skin as if the light of the sun had been switched off.

"Mitchell," she said, her tone aloof. "I'm almost done. If Veronica returns, tell her I'm indisposed for the moment and will return."

My intel was correct. Mitchell was Mitchell Leonardo.

I made a mental reminder to learn more.

Madeline didn't wait for Mitchell's response before turning back toward the foyer and disappearing beyond the walls.

"Damn women," Leonardo muttered.

His tone triggered the small hairs on my neck to bristle. "Is there a problem?"

"Better not be."

I reached into my pocket and removed a money clip. Pulling a ten-dollar bill from the clip, I laid it upon the bar near my water. No, it didn't cost ten dollars for water. In reality it was free. "Thank you, Tina," I said with a nod. "I will see you this evening."

"Thank you," she said, gathering the glass and her tip. "It won't be me. I'll be home with the family."

"Lucky you." With that I exited the bar. To my right were the doors leading me to the street. It was the direction I should go. I didn't.

The ladies' room wasn't as far away on the first floor as it had been on the second. And unlike upstairs, it wasn't as secluded. My gaze went this way and that as I made my way closer to where I believed Madeline had gone. With each step, my heart beat faster as anticipation for the future combined with memories of last night.

My need was palpable, gnawing at my nerves until my fingers itched to touch her, my lips ached to kiss her, and my arms flexed to hold her.

My desire was to see her alone, if only for a moment. While my body had its own set of goals, my mind wanted something simpler, yet at the same time more difficult to accomplish. I would take this opportunity to try to explain that I was suddenly in the tournament. While I couldn't divulge the real reason— that I was part of Sparrow and we were concerned about Antonio Hillman's reappearance—I could at least warn her of my impending presence.

Thankfully, due to the time of day, like the whole of the club, the hallways were mostly empty. They were completely empty on the way to the ladies' room. I hadn't passed a soul. At the door, I hesitated. I could wait outside as I'd done last night. However, if

I did and we spoke in the hallway, there was always the chance Mitchell would come looking for her.

Taking the chance that Madeline was alone and the only occupant of the ladies' room, I slowly pushed the door inward and peered inside.

She didn't notice me at first. With the length of her coat covering her body, her hands had a death grip upon the vanity's edge. Not looking in the mirror, I believed her eyes were shut as her head tilted down. Her silky long dark ponytail cascaded down her back.

A quick glance under the stalls told me what I wanted to know.

We were alone.

Turning toward the hallway door, I twisted the deadbolt, assuring we wouldn't be disturbed. As the mechanism clicked, Madeline's chin snapped up, and her gaze came my way through the reflection. Immediately she spun toward me.

I don't know what I expected to see, but it wasn't what I saw.

Hurt, anger, and maybe even rage radiated from her green eyes as Madeline stared my direction.

My mind tried to make rhyme or reason out of her misplaced emotion. While I contemplated the cause, she placed her hands on her hips.

"You son of a bitch. You have some nerve following me in here."

MADELINE

*a*s Patrick's blue eyes swirled with uncertainty, I stood taller. Though my array of emotions threatened my facade, my voice came out determined and hushed. "Say something."

Patrick stood silent, taking me in, scanning me from my tied-back hair to my high-heeled boots. With each passing second, his head shook. Finally, he came closer, step by step, his loafers tapping across the tile floor.

Dressed again in an expensive suit with a crisp white shirt, today he was also wearing a tie. Silver in color, it was similar to the dress I'd worn last night. Peering from beneath the cuffs of his suit jacket, black onyx cufflinks shimmered under the harsh bathroom lights. The closer he came, the more the aroma of his spicy cologne filled my senses as the sky blue of his eyes zeroed in on me.

Fuck him.

Last night, I listened to my desires. I'd let my body make

decisions. Today my head was in control. Today I had more at stake.

"Madeline, I'm sorry I left you. I needed—"

My palm swung forward.

Patrick reared backward as my hand collided with his cheek and the sound of a slap echoed against the walls.

Before I could retrieve it, my wrist was seized. "What the hell, Madeline?"

"I should have known," I said, freeing his grasp of me. "I should have known you didn't come to my room last night for me." I took a step back and did a slow spin.

"What are you talking about?"

I began speaking as soon as our eyes again met. "I'm just curious, have you already cashed in my chips? Forty thousand will be a nice addition to your play tonight."

"You know about me playing?" he asked. "How do you know that? I just..." His handsome face tilted. "What were you saying about your chips?"

"As if you don't know." I took a deep breath. "Get out of my way, Patrick. You were right that we never divorced. We will rectify that as soon as possible. I don't know why it was never done," I said. "Maybe in the back of my mind I wanted to have the illusion that there was still one man in the world who cared for me, even if it was a long time ago. Maybe I wanted the memory of someone trustworthy and honorable." I stood taller. "I suppose I should thank you for the reality check."

He stepped closer, reaching for my upper arms. Even through the coat and sweater, his grasp tightened as our eyes stayed fixed. His deep tone reverberated. "I have no idea why you are so upset. I don't know a damn thing about your chips. How the hell would I? And, Madeline, you're right; I'm not a good man. I never claimed to be. Not when we were stealing food and picking pockets and sure as hell not now. I do things I'd never want you to know. I am, however, trustworthy and honorable to those I care for."

I looked from side to side at his large hands holding on to either arm. I wanted to tell him what I'd told Mitchell. I wanted to say not to touch me. Wanting to say it and meaning it were not the same thing.

I pushed the words away. Instead, I looked back up at his blue eyes and repeated what he'd said. "People you care for...was I ever one of those? I mean, I get that I'm not now. I don't deserve to be. But tell me, was I?"

His grip tightened as he pulled me closer, my boots stuttering over the tile until our bodies became flush.

It was probably the long winter coat, but damn, the temperature was rising.

I concentrated on the most important thing: this man stole from me. I lifted my chin. "Was I?" I asked again.

"Do you need to ask?"

"I thought—"

My sentence disappeared, swallowed as his lips took mine.

Such as it had been last night, the connection was instantaneous. With only a kiss, like a spark to my dry soul, Patrick ignited a flame inside me. In mere seconds, he took my words, my thoughts, and my breath...

I longed to lean toward him, to give.

No.

No.

It was too late for that.

Along with my handbag, Patrick had taken my trust.

I pulled away, breaking his grasp. My neck straightened as I worked to recreate the mask I wore during play, the one I wore with Andros and others in the Ivanov bratva, the one of indifference. "I don't know what you know about me, the me I am today," I clarified. "I don't know how or why I became your mark, but let me say that it won't happen again. I will win tonight, tomorrow afternoon, and Saturday night. The winnings and the jackpot will be mine. I will do that because I have no other option."

"Maddie, I'm sorry. I can't say much. I can't make any of this make sense or explain the whys. Just trust me that there is more happening here than you know. When the tournament ends, you won't be the champion."

"You bought in. Is that what you can't say?"

"You knew that. That's what you'd said," Patrick replied. "Besides, my presence in the tournament wouldn't have been a secret for long. Tonight you would have seen me. When our paths crossed this afternoon, I followed you to warn you and explain."

"Explain what, Patrick? Explain that you want to stop me from doing what I do, what I do to live and survive. Why? Do you hate me for not returning years ago? Is this revenge?"

"Hate you? I fucking should."

Swallowing, I nodded.

"I should, but I don't. This tournament isn't about you. My God, if it were, I would be your biggest supporter. What you've entered is bigger than you and me. It's..." He took a deep breath. "Like I said, it's *more*." His eyes opened wide. "You just said that this is what you do to survive. Maddie, if you need money, I can help you. The jackpot is different. It's..." His nostrils flared as he exhaled. "No matter what, you won't be the champion. It will not happen. However, if it's money you need, I will give it to you, no strings attached."

I huffed. "There is no such thing. I know that all too well. Besides why would I believe you after what you did?"

Patrick took a step back. "You're upset because I left this morning without waking you?" He didn't let me answer before he continued. "I wanted to stay. I did. God, leaving your bed and your hotel room was one of the hardest things I've ever done in my entire life."

My head shook.

"I don't know why you don't believe me," he went on. "I wanted to stay. I want to stay. I want to have you beside me every damn night and wake by you every morning."

"You're not a good liar. You never have been."

"Because," he said, his voice growing louder, "I'm not fucking lying. Do you know exactly how many women I've made a commitment to, one that includes forever? Do you?"

"And have you stolen from this long list of women?"

His forehead furrowed. "It's not a long list, and what the hell would I steal? The only thing I want from you is you."

I exhaled as I paced to the stalls and back. "It seems the one thing you want isn't available."

"You said there wasn't someone else."

"I said I never married...again," I added. "I said a lot of things. None of it matters. Nothing will matter if I don't do what I came here to do." My eyes narrowed. "Are you going to cheat, Patrick? Is that how you know you will win?"

"No, Maddie. I will win because that was what I have been

tasked with doing. And I repeat, it has nothing to do with you or most of the others in the tournament. It is beyond all of our control."

My head shook. "Oh hell no. There have been many things out of my control. I've fought my way back and this..." I gestured around. "...this tournament is in my control. And I will do it. I have already taken care of the chips, so if your goal was to make me forfeit, it failed. That attempt failed, just as your plan to win will fail. I will advance. I will be sitting at the table on Saturday night. If you're there, bring it on, Mr. Kelly. You've been warned—I will win."

"Why do you keep bringing up your chips?"

The door rattled on its hinges. "Ms. Miller, Madeline," Veronica's voice came from the other side.

"Just a minute." I exhaled as I lowered my voice. "May we please avoid this uncomfortable situation? Let me leave and make an excuse for the locked door. Wait for a few minutes and then you can leave."

"Maddie, I don't know a damn thing about your chips."

I waved my hand. "Goodbye. Don't come see me again. The man I remembered is gone. It's time I live in reality. I don't know you, Mr. Kelly. I don't know if I ever did." I lifted a finger, silently asking for his compliance.

With sadness in his expression, he nodded and stepped to where the door would hide his presence.

I took a deep breath and opened the door. "Veronica, I apologize. I needed a moment."

Together Veronica and I walked down the hallway toward the foyer. Before we reached the archway, she handed me a new receipt. "Here, this will match the one you were given last night.

We have decided to increase one of the tables to seven players. It's an acceptable number. No one who arrives this evening will be eliminated. However, as stated, only eighteen will advance from tonight's play."

I looked down at the receipt in my grasp. "Thank you, Veronica. I won't mention what we discussed. You can believe me."

"I'm still cheering for you."

I let out a long breath and turned. Mitchell was waiting in the foyer, his coat draped over his arm. Once we were in the taxi, I simply said, "The receipt isn't an issue. The chips are secure and I can get another key at the desk."

"Maybe the phone fell out of your purse in the taxi last night?"

I turned toward Mitchell as a smile came to my face. "Are you actually helping me?"

"No, I'm helping me. It's nearly three in the afternoon. You and I spent the day trying to track it down. At least it's dead. It can't be traced. It's a long shot, but the boss may go for it."

"Thank you, Mitchell."

We remained silent until we entered the hotel. Thankfully, the woman at the front desk was not the same person as last night. Once we reached my room, I inserted the new key. As the door beeped, I didn't even try to stop Mitchell's entry. He was a step behind me.

Both of us stopped at the sight before us. My eyes opened wider in disbelief.

Fuck.

PATRICK

"*B*eckman bristled some, but he knew he was between a rock and a hard place," I said, talking to Sparrow, Reid, and Mason.

Sparrow nodded. "What have we learned about Hillman?"

"He's staying at the Four Seasons. Lake view executive suite, three suites," Reid said.

"He's not coming alone," Sparrow assessed. "I want Sparrows everywhere. Fucking get them on the hotel floor if you can. I want to know what he's doing every minute. Can you get his room bugged?"

"I can," I volunteered. "I have a crew waiting for just that. The thing is, you know his men will sweep. They'll take out every camera or recording device. The placement will be us welcoming him to town. His removing them will be his fuck you back."

Sparrow's dark eyes blinked shut. "It was fucking easier when no one was the wiser. Hillman's dad would never have looked for some of the high-tech shit we have today."

"That's why he's rotting in jail along with McFadden," Reid said. "Patrick's right. My advice is to have the crews flying low, both at the club and the hotel."

"The club?" I asked. "I'll be there."

"Concentrating on the cards, I hope," Sparrow replied. "You can't do it all. Mason is going to be your shadow. You work on winning, and Mason will watch Hillman and Elliott."

I let out a long breath. "With me in the tournament, there are thirty-one instead of thirty. It's not a big deal, but—"

"It means thirteen will be eliminated instead of twelve," Reid volunteered.

"It also will make a difference in the cards," I said. "With seven players versus six, the cards are spread thinner. Chances of getting the one or ones you need are diminished. There's a better chance for it to fall to someone else."

"I'll tell Beckman to put you at a table of six," Sparrow said.

"He will," I replied. "I already took care of that when we discussed the buy-in. My guess is Elliott and Hillman will also be at tables of six." I couldn't say that it was Madeline who I was worried about. Most tournaments had six people. She was used to that.

Would having seven players complicate her winning?

Maybe it would be better for her to be eliminated tonight. Having her out of the tournament would be better for my concentration, but if she were eliminated, she might leave town. I didn't want that either.

Reid's deep voice brought me back to the subject at hand. "...watching the security at the Four Seasons. I'll tap into the hallway of their rooms. All three of the rooms are near one another. I also found out that Elliott is staying at the Waldorf Astoria."

"Not far from the Four Seasons," Sparrow said.

"Yeah, I thought of that," Reid said. "It could be a coincidence."

"Or it might not be," I said.

"The Waldorf is old," Reid went on. "Their security doesn't measure up for the price tag. It's easy to access. You know there aren't many places in this city I can't see."

"Unfortunately, one of those places is Club Regal," Mason said.

"Yeah," Reid agreed. "Private clubs around the city are dark. They work to keep them that way. I can watch who comes and goes from the street or alley, but that's about it. Keeping their members' activities hidden makes people freer with their money and inhibitions. If the members know for certain that what happens within those walls stays within those walls, they're more likely to patronize."

"Are you watching any other hotels?" I asked, curious about the Palmer House. "If this is McFadden's money, there could be more." I didn't fucking want him to see me enter or leave, but there was a bigger picture than Madeline. She might come first for me, but Chicago came first for Sparrow.

"We have Sparrows flying low around all the high-end hotels," Sparrow said. "They're keeping their eyes peeled. The big finale of the tournament is tomorrow night. Tonight is for observing and figuring out who is in our city."

The four of us spent the next few hours going over the reports that had been collected from the capos. There had been some increased activity at the shipyards. It could be nothing or it could be related. It might not be related and still be the tip of an iceberg. A few of the gangs near the South Side were reporting increased activity.

Hillman had arrived. He and his entourage flew into a private airport west of the city.

"He's not trying to stay under the radar," Mason said. "I don't like it."

"It seems out of character," I added. "McFadden's men had perfected the art of ruling from behind the veil."

"They needed to with McFadden's position," Sparrow said, now pacing back and forth.

Rubio McFadden was involved in government. The veil of secrecy was essential.

"What about Elliott?" Sparrow asked.

"He arrived by private jet, too," Reid confirmed. "However, it's his modus operandi. Big oil money with all the luxuries that come with it."

Ruling and running the Sparrow world was a juggling act. It always was—every day, every hour. Sometimes there were only three balls; other times there were ten. Right now it felt like fifteen. I presumed it was my new obsession with Madeline, but something about this felt different.

Too many balls.

Not enough hands.

That was ridiculous because for the last six months or more, we'd had more hands than we had during the takeovers. We had Mason back where he belonged. Nevertheless, I couldn't shake the feeling.

Reid looked down at his watch where a message had just

beeped in. Looking up, he asked, "Patrick, are you worried about the tournament?"

"I'd rather be watching."

"You've got this, man," Sparrow said.

"That message was from Lorna," Reid said. "She has dinner ready. I'm going to eat and then come back here and get the different hotel security cameras infiltrated and recording. I'll also keep a close eye on Club Regal from the outside." He looked my way. "You're welcome to join us for dinner. There's always plenty."

While the four of us often met up in Sparrow and Araneae's apartment with Lorna, Reid's wife, and Laurel, Mason's wife, for breakfast, dinner was more spread out. It gave each person a bit of freedom. "Nah, I'm going to clean up and grab dinner at Club Regal. I figure I need to make my presence known." I turned to Mason. "You want to come with me?"

"I'm going to eat here with Laurel. She's been gone for the last few evenings. Something is happening with her research, making her cautiously excited. Hell, I didn't think it possible, but she's sleeping less than me. I wake and she's in the office reading and running equations. I consider myself pretty smart, but damn, I don't have a clue." He scoffed. "I'm glad she's excited. I want to hear what's been happening."

I nodded. "I hate that you have to leave her to babysit me at the club."

"Not babysitting. I'm just your extra set of eyes."

I probably needed it, but not for the reason everyone thought.

He patted my shoulder. "I'll clean up too, and be to Club

Regal before they assign the seats. You watch the cards and keep up your earnings. I'll keep an eye on the room."

"Okay," I smirked. "Cleaning up might not be a bad idea." I eyed his blue jeans, t-shirt, and colorful arms. Not everyone felt the need to wear a suit every day. My gaze went to his hair longer than ours. His hung past his chin, a far cry from the haircuts we'd had in the army. While the buzz cut stuck with me, it didn't with Mason. "How about a haircut?"

Mason laughed. "I'll see you at the club." He stopped. "I want a list of all thirty-one players and their most recent picture and biography. That way I'll know who everyone is."

I nodded, looking at Reid. "I can pull it up so you can get to Lorna."

"I can do it. It will only take seconds."

Of course it would.

I stood, stretching my arms over my head. The suit coat from earlier was gone and the sleeves were rolled up on my shirt. It wasn't that I didn't do casual. It was that I didn't do it often.

Sparrow and I walked toward the steel door. He laid his hand on the sensor. A moment later we were waiting for the elevator.

"Is there something else?" Sparrow asked.

"What?"

"I can't put my finger on it. Should I have assigned playing in the tournament to someone else?"

My stomach twisted. I didn't lie to these men. I would risk my life for any one of them. We knew one another's darkest secrets. Maybe that was the thing. Maybe to me, Madeline hadn't been a dark secret, but a light one. A ray of sunshine that while gone, reminded me what it had been like to have someone special, someone like these other men had found. Exposing her now would darken that memory in a way I wasn't prepared to do.

Not yet.

"Nah," I said as we stepped into the elevator. I hit A for the floor with the apartments while Sparrow hit P. "I'm just thinking about all of it. Hillman's brazen move bothers me. I can't decide if Elliott is an issue or not. And then there are the other players in the tournament. I'm worried there's more I'm not seeing."

The elevator stopped on A.

Sparrow reached out to hold the door open. "You're right."

I looked at my friend and boss. "I am? About what?"

"I'll have Reid run background checks on the other players in the tournament. Maybe we're too focused on Hillman to see what is right in front of us."

Shit.

That wasn't exactly what I'd wanted.

I didn't say that. Instead, I nodded. "Don't worry. I'll win tonight."

"I'm not," Sparrow said with a grin as he released his grip and disappeared behind the closing door.

MADELINE

I couldn't believe my eyes. The bed was made, the room picked up. Those were things I'd expected. That wasn't what had my attention. Sitting on the bedside stand was my handbag. Beside it was my phone, plugged into the charger. I turned from the sight to Mitchell. His eyes were equally as wide.

"Go," he said, nodding toward the bag, "check the contents."

The bathroom door, the one we'd passed without thought, opened.

I let out the tiniest of gasps as my neck straightened.

In the doorway was a man I knew too well. His presence dwarfed Mitchell's. It wasn't necessarily physical presence. It was obvious that this man was in better shape, his muscles more defined, but he was an inch or two shorter. However, his height didn't detract from his omnipotent power that emanated from him as Mitchell and I both took a step back.

"Andros."

"Boss."

Our greetings came simultaneously.

Ignoring, Mitchell, Andros set his sights on me.

The black button-down shirt he wore was unbuttoned at the collar with his sleeves rolled up to near his elbows and tucked into the trim waist of his black slacks that covered his long legs. With each step forward, his dark eyes probed my gaze for answers I couldn't give.

Closer and closer he came until he reached up, cupping my cheek.

My flinch was involuntary, almost going unseen.

Almost.

His face tilted as his thumb ran gently over my cheekbone, inspecting his latest marking. "Mitchell, leave us."

I wanted to send Mitchell a silent plea to stay.

How crazy was it that I wanted him near when in reality I hated him too?

Nevertheless, I couldn't pull my stare away from Andros. Doing so would be considered a rebuttal. Those didn't occur concerning Andros without consequences. I could thank Andros for my lessons on remaining calm and indifferent. I'd learned them well and they helped me in poker as well as everyday life. The slightest twitch or change of expression could be easily misconstrued. Verbally disagreeing would be even worse.

The door to the hallway opened and closed, only the audible noises giving me the intel as I continued staring unblinkingly at Andros Ivanov.

"My dear, what have you done to cause you to fear me?"

My head shook. "I'm not afraid. I'm surprised." It was a bald-faced lie and we both knew it.

"Ah," he said with a grin as he leaned closer and his lips came to my other cheek. The combination of coffee, whiskey, and overpowering cologne filled my senses. The mixture was a catalyst increasing the dread bubbling within my stomach.

Exhaling, I took a step back, and reached for the buttons on my coat. My tone was a forced one of lightheartedness. "What brings you to Chicago?"

"There is business at hand but none as significant as you."

After removing it, I laid my coat over the back of one of the chairs. As I did, my purse and phone across the room again caught my attention. "Is that...?" I nodded toward the bedside stand. "...I thought I'd lost it."

"And yet you didn't tell me."

Casually, I walked past the mountain of a man and nonchalantly opened the handbag. My entire body relaxed as I worked to stifle my sigh of relief. Everything was as I'd last seen it. The receipt, my identification, my credit cards, and even the cash were all in place. The only thing missing was the phone, and that wasn't missing but lying beside it.

I let out a breath and turned to Andros. "I was embarrassed. I told you I was looking for it. I fell asleep last night not even realizing it was missing, or so I thought. Where...?"

"It was here when I walked in. The purse was lying on the bed."

"And you opened it?"

"To check for your phone. After all, it needed charging."

"Yes," I said with a nod. "Of course. Thank you."

"Tell me, Madeline, do you have secrets within the handbag or maybe the phone that you don't want me to know?"

"No, Andros. How could I have secrets from you?"

"That's what I wonder too."

I gestured around the hotel room. "I don't have anything to offer you except water. I could call for room service. Wine? Something stronger?"

"So accommodating." His smile grew. "You've learned your place well. Isn't that so?"

The condescension in his statement added to my unease. It was part of his power play. Thankfully, I'd learned to play.

Lifting my chin, I met his gaze. "Yes, Andros. You're a marvelous teacher." When the silence built, I asked, "May I ask about how——?"

"Our concentration is here with your job at hand," he interrupted.

"Yes, of course. Are you staying?" I looked around. "Here?" Our gazes again met. "With me? Are you coming to the tournament?"

"I couldn't be away from you."

I had no idea what was happening or why he was here, but I would place money on it having less to do with a yearning to be near me and more about something else—something bigger.

Wasn't that what Patrick had said?

How could Patrick possibly know about Andros Ivanov?

Patrick.

Oh my God!

The realization twisted a knife in my chest. Patrick hadn't taken my purse. I'd thought the worst of him—I'd accused him. No wonder he'd been perplexed. I couldn't think about that now.

I looked back to Andros. "So you will stay?"

"Not here." He looked around with an air of superiority.

"Are there people here—at the tournament—that you want to see?" I shouldn't ask, but curiosity was difficult to ignore. "Hillman or Elliott?"

Andros's chin rose. "I thought you weren't charmed. Was that not true?"

I shook my head. "I'm not."

"Yet you mention his name. Tell me, how can I trust you when you lied to me about the phone and purse? You said you fell asleep and when you woke you thought you'd left it somewhere. And when I enter, it is here."

"It wasn't. I checked."

"How would it disappear and reappear?"

"I don't know. Mitchell and I both thought it was missing. He took me back to the club to see if it was there. We called the taxi company."

"So Mitchell is involved with your deception?"

"No, not deception," I corrected. "I asked him to give me time. I didn't want to disappoint you." I went to the handbag. Opening it, I pulled out the receipt. "I was afraid this was gone. I knew you'd be angry."

"Remove your sweater."

My steps stuttered backward as I pushed the receipt back into the handbag. "Excuse me?"

His chin rose yet his expression was granite and unchanging. "My orders don't require explanations nor contemplation."

I lifted my fingers to the row of buttons that ran from the neckline to the hem. "I just don't understand." Tears prickled the back of my eyes. The dread I'd felt at his unexpected arrival came back to life as I did as he'd warned against. I contemplated.

What were his plans?

While my fingers began to unfasten, my eyes closed and I considered my options. There were none. I couldn't escape the hotel room and definitely not Chicago. It wouldn't matter if I could. I wouldn't and Andros knew that.

Tugging the length from the waist of my slacks, I exposed my bra.

Was I exposing more?

Were there visible signs of my union with Patrick last night?

I couldn't think about that possibility as I removed the sweater and laid it upon the bed.

"Lovely." Andros's compliment was overflowing with saccharine, artificial sweetness. "Turn around."

One breath in. I swallowed and complied.

When I had made a full circle, he again spoke. "Tsk. That won't do. Remove your bra too."

"Andros...please. I don't know what you want."

In two steps he was in front of me, staring down. "But you do. I told you."

My fingers fumbled with the clasps behind my back. I unfastened the clasps and began pulling the straps from my shoulders and down my arms. Once it was free, Andros took it from my grasp and inspected the lace. I wanted to ask what he was doing and why he was doing it.

I didn't.

"You are a beautiful woman, Madeline. No wonder Marion Elliott is interested."

Knowing better than to cover myself, I kept my arms at my sides. "I'm not. I'm not interested in Marion Elliott. Please believe me."

"What happened with your purse?"

My skin was now flushed with goose bumps as Andros's timbre slowed. It was an ominous precursor I'd learned to heed. "I don't know. I don't. I searched for it this morning when Mitchell woke me. I couldn't find it. There was no other explanation than that I'd lost it last night. We went to the club. I spoke to Veronica. You can ask her. I was there. I was worried about the chip receipt and my place in the tournament if the purse couldn't be found. She provided me with a new receipt. It's in my coat pocket. I can show it to you." My sentences were coming faster and faster as each one left my lips.

I turned toward the bedside stand. "Maybe..." I searched for any possibility. "Maybe the maid found it when she cleaned the room." My eyes widened. "Yes, that makes sense. I thought I searched thoroughly, but maybe I didn't. Maybe it had fallen. Yes, under the bed. I was too upset to check as thoroughly as I should have done. It's here. That's all that matters."

Andros came closer, his stare again zeroed in on mine. The tips of his fingers skirted my cheek, sending cold chills down my spine. The chills scurried like tiny insects avoiding a known threat. His touch continued to move, down my neck and to my shoulder. All at once, his fingers entwined in the length of my ponytail and yanked my head backward. The ceiling disappeared as his face materialized within inches of mine. "Is *that* all that matters?"

"No," I managed to answer. "I'm sorry I didn't find the purse." Tears were now escaping my eyes. "Andros, please. I have the tournament."

"It's true." His free hand again went to my cheek. "Perhaps not such a visible reminder of who you belong to."

"I don't need a reminder. I've been here as you said and with Mitchell. I know who." The words churned my stomach as another name came to mind, one I tried unsuccessfully to forget. It was the name of a man who didn't need to show his strength in ways like this.

"Tell me."

"You. Andros. It's you."

He released my ponytail, giving instant relief to my scalp.

"Turn around, Madeline. I want your hands on the bed."

The relief evaporated as I complied, my mind a mix of what was to come. My breasts were exposed, but I was still wearing my slacks and boots. He hadn't instructed me to remove them. This wasn't sex.

Or maybe?

My breathing caught and blood ran cold as I heard Andros unlatch his belt.

"It pains me to need to do this."

My head fell forward as I prepared for what was to come.

"Your slacks."

Standing straighter, my fingers trembled as I unlatched the thin belt and the button and lowered the zipper. Before they fell, I looked up. "Andros, please." It was then I realized his belt was in his grasp, fully removed from the loops, yet his trousers were still fastened.

As crazy as it sounded, there was instant relief knowing this wouldn't be sex.

Would it have been?

Sex was consensual. Whatever Andros planned was about power. Rape was also about power.

I turned and placed my hands back on the bed allowing the

slacks to fall to the carpet, revealing my panties as I prayed for one lash.

Who does that?

Who had I become?

One was sustainable.

"Six," his one-word sentence sent shivers scurrying down my spine.

"Six?"

"The number of calls you missed."

The knowledge added to my dread.

Six.

Could I take it?

I had but not before a public appearance.

I held my breath, my muscles growing taut even knowing that the tenseness would make it worse.

My eyes closed and lip disappeared between my teeth as I prepared for the strike. I wouldn't beg any more. I wouldn't display the emotion he sought. Andros's power wasn't innate; people gave it to him by submitting to his demands. I'd given him all I could. There was nothing left. I braced myself.

Silence prevailed. Until it was sliced open by the split-second whistle. My body tensed.

The leather landed on the bed near my hand.

"Stand up, Madeline."

With my entire body trembling, I stood. This time he cupped my chin as his thumb wiped away tears from both cheeks. "I believe you."

"Oh..." I released the breath I'd been holding.

His hand came to my shoulder. "Tonight...you will answer."

It wasn't a question; nevertheless, I replied, "Yes, Andros, I will answer."

His touch disappeared. "Dress."

Nodding, I reached for my bra. As I fumbled again with my shaking fingers, Andros tapped my shoulder, turning me, and clasped the latches. "Thank you," I whispered.

"Your honesty earned your reprieve."

I pulled up my slacks and began buttoning the sweater.

"And Mitchell, for his role?" he asked.

"Are you asking me?"

"Yes, my dear. If the blame doesn't lie with you, where does it lie?"

"Not with him." I couldn't believe my words. Less than twenty-four hours ago I had threatened to kill him myself and now I was defending him. "Me before him," I said, feigning strength I knew was lost. "I asked him for time to find it to avoid disappointing you. The blame lies with me."

I tucked the sweater back into my slacks and fastened the belt. "Thank you for believing me."

"I have a job for you. Tell me you will not let me down, not again."

"No, of course, Andros. I'll do whatever you want."

"Very good. I'll have food delivered. Shower and prepare yourself for the tournament."

Andros went to my closet and opened the doors. As he did, the light within shone down on the rack. He hummed aloud as his large hand grazed over the dresses within, all very expensive and purchased with his money. Reaching for a long black silk one with the tags still attached, he removed it from the closet.

"This will do."

I'd only tried it on once. It was one of the most sought-after fashions of late. I took the hanger, reading the tag: *Sinful Threads*. I didn't say a word as I ran my hand over the luxurious silk.

"And your hair, wear it up. And the emerald jewelry..." He lifted my chin. "Yes, it will match your eyes."

My nerves were frayed as I worked to suppress my trepidation. "What do you want me to do?"

"*Who*, my dear. New information has come to light. The question isn't what but who." His fingertip came to my lips. "I want you to be you. This will be your favor to me. This will work to my benefit." Again he caressed my cheek. "He won't be able to take his eyes off you."

PATRICK

*a*s I entered Club Regal, for the first time since seeing Madeline last night, my mind was not on her but on the job at hand. I agreed with the Sparrows—there was something brewing that needed to be squelched.

That being said, I wasn't thrilled about spending my night counting cards and calculating the odds. That wouldn't be all I did. I would also watch my opponents. The way the tournament worked was advancement came through winnings, not gross but net for the night. The initial stack was subtracted at the end of play.

I could win every pot at my assigned table and still not make the cut. The accumulated earnings had to be substantial in order to rank in one of the top eighteen spots for the night.

Each night began again.

Yes, I would start with a substantial stack of chips as did everyone else. What mattered was the difference at the end of the night. I wasn't certain of the amount of earnings Madeline had accumulated the first night. When enough players end up in the red, even a small margin of profit can be enough.

That was what I was going for tonight—enough.

I told myself that tonight's play was only the first step. I needed to win enough to make it to the top eighteen and whether it was egotistical or not, I wasn't concerned. My concern was focused elsewhere.

Hillman especially.

It would be interesting to see how Antonio reacted to my presence, not only as an overseeing figure, but as a contender. I didn't give a shit how he or anyone else felt. I wasn't present to make friends.

That wasn't completely true. I cared about Madeline, and from our brief encounter earlier this afternoon, I knew that she wasn't happy.

What I couldn't figure out were her comments about her chips.

I had too many things to consider. That didn't mean I wouldn't learn more tonight. If I didn't discover my answers here at the club, I sure as hell would tonight back in her hotel room. I still had her key and planned to use it.

The two of us needed to talk, and I needed answers.

After leaving my outer coat at coat check, I adjusted my suit coat and tie and entered Bar Regal. Near the center of the connecting rooms, a man in a tuxedo tickled the keys of the grand piano filling the air with melodies. The music was subtle yet lively, the perfect backdrop as the evening's festivities moved into high gear. Not everyone present was here for the tournament. No, Bar Regal as well as the cigar room and restaurant were filling to capacity. After all, it was Friday night.

"Mr. Kelly," a woman's voice came from behind me.

Turning, I grinned as one of the hardworking managers of Club Regal came my direction. "Ms. Standish. It's nice to see you."

She leaned in and kissed my cheek. I politely returned the gesture. While she was a woman older than I, she was attractive with her short blonde hair and unusually high cheekbones. She was also vital to the running of this club.

"Mr. Kelly, please call me Veronica."

"Veronica," I repeated, not offering her the same informality. As part of the Sparrow upper regime, formality had its place.

Her expression turned serious. "I want you to know that I hold no ill will about your entering the tournament."

"That's nice to hear." I wasn't certain why she would. After all Hillman had been afforded the opportunity. Instead of saying that, I added, "I do realize it's unusual."

She forced a smile. "Creating this situation was our doing, not yours. We opened the door. I just hope it won't reflect poorly upon Club Regal when it's time to bid on future tournaments. I'm certain Mr. Sparrow would not be happy if we were unable to attract the high rollers."

"Veronica, I'll be happy to let him know of your concern. Since my entering the tournament was his idea, I'm sure he won't mind that you're second-guessing his decisions."

"No," she answered quickly. "That isn't..." Her hand came to my sleeve. "I respect Mr. Sparrow's decisions as does Mr. Beckman. Your entry isn't the one I'm concerned about."

Hillman's?

Why?

I peered over her head and around, wondering if we were

being overheard. "If you have something to tell me, something you believe Mr. Sparrow should know, please feel free." I leaned closer. "Perhaps a more private venue is recommended."

She shook her head as her lips pursed. "I have nothing more to say. As it is, I've said too much. I trust you, Mr. Sparrow, and your associates to make it right, to keep things as they are. It's been nice since—"

"Veronica," Ethan Beckman said overenthusiastically as he joined the two of us. "Mr. Kelly, welcome." For only a microsecond, he sent Veronica a silencing glance before gratuitously gesturing around the bar. "Please, Mr. Kelly, relax before the tournament. Dinner, drinks, or whatever you'd like is on the house. Nothing but the best to help calm the nerves. We hope you enjoy your tournament play this evening."

"Thank you," I said. "My nerves are fine. However, when it comes to hospitality, Ms. Standish had just offered me the same."

"She did?" he asked, looking between the two of us.

A waiter passed by with a plate of steaming shrimp scampi. "Yes," I went on, "she was telling me about the shrimp scampi." I lowered my voice. "I'm dying to know the secret ingredient, but it seems she won't tell me. I will have to give it a try and see if I can figure it out for myself."

"Yes, you must," Veronica said with a nod.

Beckman's head bobbed. "Very well. I didn't mean to interrupt the two of you."

"No, not at all," I replied. "As I said, I'm looking forward to a bite to eat before the real fun begins."

Beckman gestured again toward the bar where there were a few empty seats. "You're welcome to sit at the bar, or if you'd prefer, Mr. Kelly, I will be happy to secure you a table in the steak house."

"The bar is adequate," I said.

He walked with me to an empty stool and motioned to the bartender. "We want to make you happy."

"Thank you, Beckman. I'm confident you will."

It wasn't my happiness he was concerned about. It was Sparrow's.

Taking a breath, I lifted myself up to a stool not far from where I'd been earlier today.

"Mr. Kelly," the bartender, a young man, said. "What can we get for you tonight?"

Before I could answer, my interest was diverted to a tall table in the adjoining room, near the piano. It wasn't the table or even the piano that demanded my attention. It was the presence of the most beautiful woman I knew or had ever known. In her hand was a glass of white wine. Tonight's dress was black, sleek and shiny like her hair. The way the dress hugged her curves was vaguely familiar. It wasn't the dress but the person beneath who had me enthralled.

I'd held those curves last night. Simply the thought of it made my circulation reroute.

This wasn't the time or the place.

Yet I couldn't look away. Like a model on a runway, she had my full notice. Her raven dark hair was not down as it had been last night, but piled high on top of her head with ringlets near her cheeks. Around her neck was a large necklace, the mounting made of a dark metal, and the stones shining emeralds. It complemented her dress and showcased her vibrant green eyes.

Widening my focus, I noticed the man at her side. I recognized him from last night's play.

Why was Madeline having a drink with Marion Elliott?

"Mr. Kelly?" the bartender repeated, "may I get you a drink?"

"Blanton's, neat."

"Very well. Would you like anything else?"

The raven-haired beauty by the piano. I didn't say that. "I've heard wonderful things about your shrimp scampi. I'd like a salad first with your house dressing."

After I'd given my order, I found my attention pulled back to Madeline and her companion, Marion Elliott. As my mind filled with more questions, I had a stark realization. Marion Elliott was on the Sparrow radar. Madeline being with Elliott would put her on the same radar. It was a place I didn't want her to be.

Madeline was a gambler, a poker player. Whatever was happening did not involve her. It couldn't.

Utilizing the reflection of the large mirror behind the bar, I searched the room for Mitchell Leonardo. I hadn't had the opportunity to research him, not with others on two. Nevertheless, my gut told me that he was present to watch over Madeline. While I also got the feeling that she wasn't one of his biggest fans, he seemed to have a job with her.

Where was he and why wasn't he standing by while Madeline made nice with one of the highest rollers in the poker world?

A ruckus came from the entry, drawing everyone's attention.

Fucker wasn't trying to lie low.

I sent a text to Mason.

HILLMAN HAS ARRIVED.

MADELINE

My gaze went from the five cards in my hand to the other five players. There was only one player from my table last night, Mr. Daniels. I'd done my research and found him to be personally as boring as his online persona. I also didn't consider him to be much of a threat.

The other four players were new to me, in person. I knew their online personas by heart. However, it was in person that gave me the advantage. In our short time of play, I was deciphering my newer opponents' tells. Mr. Garcia, a local businessman, took a sip of his rum and coke each time he was unsure. A healthy hand and his glass remained untouched. Mr. Robertson, who had traveled from England where he owned manufacturing houses worth billions, was subtler. He had a very slight sway to the left when the cards fell the way he wanted, as opposed to his total statuesque stillness when they didn't. That left Dr. Bolton, a doctor from the West Coast. Some might consider him a manic, a player who does a lot of hyper-aggressive raising and betting. I hadn't decided if he was a good player or simply a gambler at heart.

What was important was that the stack of chips before me was growing.

I'd changed my strategy from last night. During our drinks, Marion Elliott had mentioned how others were talking about the lady with a bigger reputation than deserved. That didn't bother me. Let them all underestimate me. However, if I were to play with the big boys on Saturday night, I needed the tall stack, the assets that came with accumulated funds.

Keeping status quo may have allowed me to make the first cut, it might even make tonight's. However, if I continued that strategy and continued to advance, in the final round I wouldn't have the betting power to win. It went without saying that each of the final six players would come into play with a tall stack of chips.

The pretournament drinks had yielded other interesting tidbits of information. Marion ended last night's play with over two hundred grand, over 150 more than I. He hadn't mentioned it as a way to boast but more casually, as if he were surprised such a night's small earnings had landed him in the first-place spot.

He jokingly accused me and others of sandbagging. While I laughed it off, that was exactly what I had been doing. I wasn't any longer.

The current bet came to me. The ante had been five grand and so was the first bet. I could call at five grand. We still had our original five cards; there was a draw still to come.

Marion Elliott didn't accumulate two hundred grand with minuscule $5000 bets. It was time to up my game.

Flashing a smile, I moved my gaze around the table.

The hand I'd been dealt was weak, but as with any one, there was potential:

7, 8, 8, J, Q

Odds would tell me to keep the pair of eights. It could be enough. Maybe with a three-card draw I could get another pair or maybe a third eight. The riskier move was to give up the seven and eight and hope for an inside straight. I would need a nine and a ten.

I pushed five chips toward the dealer and nodded at Dr. Bolton who had placed the first bet. "I see your five." I moved ten more chips. "And raise you ten."

"Fifteen grand before the draw?" Mr. Robertson asked dismissively. "A tilt by the lady." He shoved ten grand into the pot. "I call."

It was a disparaging remark insinuating that I was playing wildly or recklessly. No doubt he believed it would throw me off my game. On the contrary, I smiled, hoping to do the same to him.

The next two players folded.

It came to Mr. Garcia. "I will see you for the draw."

Now was the moment of truth. "Cards?" the dealer asked.

Taking only two would give the illusion of three-of-a-kind. However, I wasn't here to bluff my way to the final table. I removed the 7, J, and Q, placing them facedown, said, "Three."

Mr. Robertson's shake of his head didn't go unnoticed.

I didn't reveal the new cards as the call went around the table. Mr. Robertson took two. It was Mr. Garcia who had my attention.

"I'm good." He would keep his five dealt cards.

Fuck.

What was he sitting on?

Scooping the additional three cards into my hand, I began to fan them.

8 and 8, the cards I retained.

9.

Shit.

That would have been the first for the straight.

9.

I remained calm. Two pair was a good hand. Normally, it was. However, normally a player asked for at least one card. Mr. Garcia hadn't.

The final card.

8.

I had a full house.

"Ms. Miller, I believe as the last to raise, the bet is to you," the dealer said.

I looked to Mr. Robertson who had just lowered his glass of rum and coke. He wasn't my concern. Grinning toward the table, I pushed in the appropriate chips. "I bet ten." That would be another ten grand. With my current bet, the pot was sitting at $110 grand.

Mr. Robertson was the first to withdraw. "I'll wait for another hand," he said, laying his cards facedown on the table. "I fold."

"Mr. Garcia," the dealer encouraged.

Slowly, he pushed ten more grand into the center of the table. "I'm not a selfish man, Ms. Miller, just a curious one. I will see your ten."

That meant I had to show my cards. The dealing and betting

were done.

"It's too bad you didn't push for more," I said with a smile as I turned over my full house. "Eights over nines."

"Well done." One by one he revealed his cards. A jack, another. A king, and another. The table took a collective breath as we waited. One more of either and I was beat.

His last card was an ace.

Collecting my pot, I nodded. "A kicker."

"You never know," he said with a shrug.

I should have been considering what was happening at the other tables. I should have wondered why Andros had changed his mind about Elliott. And why he wanted me to meet him for pretournament drinks. I should have wondered about Patrick. God knows I saw him enter. I even saw him momentarily at the Bar Regal before the tournament. However, with Mr. Garcia staring across the felt at me, I concentrated on what I knew.

I concentrated on cards.

Once again, I'd made it to the end of the night. My earnings were considerably more than they'd been the night before. As the dealer handed me my new receipt, I read the earnings: $510,000. I could walk away tonight with more than half of the jackpot. Or I could continue to build my earnings and walk away with those plus the jackpot.

It wasn't that I would walk away with any of it. It would belong to Andros.

My gaze caught Mitchell's as he stood in the same spot he'd been the night before. I nodded almost imperceptibly, but enough for him to see. I scanned the perimeter—the people watching, not those part of the tournament. To my surprise,

Andros wasn't there. I hadn't seen him since he'd left my hotel room after issuing my sentence, reprieve, and instructions.

He had divulged that he was staying at the Palmer House in the executive suite. He told me not to expect to see him again tonight while at the same time, not to be surprised if I did. I had been told that when he called, I would answer and deliver a full report.

"Tomorrow afternoon, the field is set at eighteen," the house announced as the room turned deadly silent. This time they began at the bottom of the list. "Number eighteen..."

As for our table, I was confident that I was either just behind Mr. Garcia or just ahead. From a distance, our stacks looked evenly paired. It would depend on what we had each brought to the table.

The numbers continued.

"Number ten, Mr. Patrick Kelly."

I sucked in a breath. He'd made the cut. I wasn't certain if the news made me happy or sad.

"Number nine, Mr. Adam Garcia."

I nodded at my tablemate. We were the only two from our table to advance.

"Congratulations," Mr. Robertson whispered.

"Number eight, Ms. Madeline Miller."

My lungs filled with air at the confirmation.

More numbers.

"Number four, Mr. Antonio Hillman."

I craned my neck to get a sight of this man, the one Andros had mentioned. I couldn't, not completely. The view was obstructed. Yet a table to my far right was congratulating him.

Three.

Two.

"Number one, Mr. Marion Elliott."

His name brought a smile to my lips. I wasn't happy for him. I was grateful.

Eight wouldn't get me to the final game. Only the top six would make it. Thankfully for me, we all began at ground zero, our only differing element the stockpile of available cash. Mine had grown considerably and like everyone else, I had one more round to move up at least two positions.

Mitchell appeared with my coat. "Ms. Miller..."

Before he could finish, Marion was standing at my side. "Madeline, we must celebrate."

The blue stare from a few tables away caused me to hesitate but only for a moment. As I turned my attention back to Marion, I lifted my hand to his and said, "We must."

PATRICK

Blood surged to my face, warming my skin, as I watched Madeline place her hand in Elliott's.

"Mr. Kelly," the dealer said, interrupting my thoughts, "here's your receipt. Congratulations, sir, on your winnings."

"Thank you," I muttered as Madeline stood and moved her hand to Elliott's bent arm. In this room of men, she was a beacon of light. The necklace around her throat glistened like the Queen's crown jewels in a glass case on display.

A large hand landed on my shoulder. I turned to see Mason standing beside me. A tall man, he could appear menacing when necessary. Tonight he'd done as he said and cleaned up, appearing almost refined. His long hair was fastened in a short ponytail at the nape of his neck. The suit he wore was custom, as nice as mine or nicer. The pointed toes of his cowboy boots made me grin. Just because they weren't Italian loafers didn't mean he hadn't spent a fortune on them. It meant, when it came to Mason, conforming wasn't his way.

"Did you see anything?" I asked.

"Yeah. Interesting dynamics. I have some theories."

The room around us was beginning to clear. Madeline and Elliott were no longer present, the same as most of the players. An exception was Antonio Hillman and his entourage. They were some of the few remaining. I stood to put my suit jacket back on, the one I'd removed during play. As I stood shoulder to shoulder with Mason, I fastened one button. Looking up, I caught the stare of the man we were sent to watch.

"It's a shame that the club's standards have dropped," Hillman said, looking our way. "There was a time this never would have been accepted. If you ask me, they need an exterminator to rid the place of birds. Filthy animals."

It would be too easy to take his bait. Refinement was a weapon men like Hillman were unable to fight against or incapable of doing so.

"Hillman," I said, standing three to four inches taller than him. "The only standard I question is your presence. I would think you'd be concerned about the optics, coming back to the scene of the crime and all."

He scoffed. "It doesn't seem to deter you. Besides, I'm here for the tournament. There's nothing illegal about that. I have no other objectives."

"Such a simple man," Mason said. "I would suppose multiple objectives would be above your skill level."

"The rumors are true," Hillman said, eyeing Mason up and down. "It's really you."

"I'm me," Mason said.

"You know what isn't true?" Hillman asked.

We didn't answer.

"The old saying that you can't kill what's already dead."

He was again baiting us, threatening Mason.

"Try it," Mason said, deadly calm.

Hillman turned back to his four henchmen. "This is boring. If memory serves me well, there's a club not too far away that my father frequented. It offered a wide variety of pleasures, all flavors, blonde, brunette, and strawberry." His men all laughed. Hillman turned back to me. "Surely Mr. Do-good hasn't rid the city of all its fun."

"He redefined the boundaries. Fun to be had must consent and be of legal age." I nodded. "Break those rules and we'll know. You're in our city."

"Enjoy the illusion." With that, he turned, his men following one on each side and two behind. Classic formation.

And he called us birds.

I pulled my phone from my pocket. "They're headed to McIver's."

"Top of the building above the Italian restaurant," Mason said in confirmation as I sent Reid a text message knowing that he'd have the place covered in Sparrows.

"I hate that place," I whispered after my text was sent and I returned my phone to my pocket.

"Yeah, after what you said happened to Araneae there, I'm surprised Sparrow didn't light it up in flames."

The boss's wife had been poisoned there before becoming his wife. Actually, at the time, she was...well, it was hard to define.

"That's the thing," I said, "Unlike those assholes, Sparrow sees the bigger picture. The city must function. He isn't out to stop that. He just makes sure it does so on his terms. Besides, the guilty parties in that incident were identified and dealt with accordingly. No need to torch the whole basket for a few bad apples."

Apple.

The perfect red apple tattoo came to mind.

"Mr. Kelly, Mr. Pierce, we must lock the room."

Mason and I nodded as we stepped out into the nearly empty landing.

"You did well tonight," Mason said. "Top ten. I was watching all five tables. The betting was getting higher and higher. There's a lot of money in that room."

"Do you think that's what it's about, the money? Do you think the tournament is all that's happening, that it *is* the bigger picture, or do you think it's a ruse?"

"I think there's more. It's a part, but not the whole picture. Even if it's a ruse," Mason said, "it is a piece of the puzzle."

His comment reminded me of what Veronica Standish had said. I had the feeling she was trying to tell me something. "I think I want to track down Veronica Standish."

"Why?"

I shrugged. "Gut, man."

"Okay." He looked around. With the exception of a few Club Regal staff passing by, we were now alone in this second-story hallway. "Hillman is an ass and a showman. He was manic in his play. Big bets. Big wins and losses, all with flair."

"He wants us to watch him."

"Which begs the question, why?" Mason said. "The way he's commanding the spotlight feels like instead of the lead, he's a distraction for someone else."

"Elliott?"

"So far we've found nothing to indicate he's any more or less than he appears, a stereotypical old Texas oilman. I was surprised to see him without a ten-gallon hat. I'm not saying our research made it look like he's a choirboy. He has been around for a long time. He's neck-deep in muck and dirty dealings all in the name of pursuing the American dream."

"It's worked well for us," I said. "I'm not one to judge."

"His is a lot of shit with emissions and drilling rights. He's greased the hands of many politicians and has the bankroll to show for it."

"McFadden?" I asked.

Before his fall from grace, Rubio McFadden was a senator. First a state senator and then he moved on to the United States Senate. His ambition was the White House. Even though he was from Illinois, that didn't mean he hadn't influenced votes that could have benefitted Marion Elliott.

"I could send that theory to Reid," Mason said, looking down at his watch, "and stay here with you."

"No need. Hillman is gone. I'd bet Reid already has him tracked on traffic cams. Maybe McIver's was another diversion. Reid will know where Hillman goes and send the appropriate Sparrows. That leaves Elliott." Who was last seen with my wife. "I will hang around and see what happens. I'm going to look for Ms. Standish and watch Elliott. You can go home."

"My job is here with you."

"I don't need a babysitter. It's late." The tournament ended play at eleven o'clock. "Go home. Instead of giving the mission to Reid, you can run a check on any McFadden-Elliott connection, and then when you're satisfied, crawl in bed with your wife. Tomorrow's another day."

We were now walking toward the stairs.

"You drive a hard bargain."

Not really. I planned on bedding my wife too. I didn't say that.

"If you learn anything else, no matter how late, send a text," Mason said.

"Will do." I waited as he retrieved his outer coat from the coat check. Once he was gone, I turned toward Bar Regal. "Where are you, Mrs. Kelly?"

MADELINE

*I*t was nearly one in the morning by the time Mitchell delivered me to my hotel room. As it had been the night before, the drapes were drawn, the lights on, and my bed was turned down with a green mint upon the pillow. Unlike the night before, the first thing I did tonight was plug my phone into the charger and verify that the ringer was on. I was ready for my call from Andros.

Experience was a strict educator. And while I wasn't above making mistakes, I rarely repeated them. If life within Andros's world was my teacher, I was its star pupil.

The truth was that I had things to tell him. While I had no doubt that Mitchell had already reported my advancement in the tournament, I wanted to give him the specifics. I was proud of my winnings thus far.

Moving from nineteenth to eighth in the rankings was an exemplary accomplishment. The world might call what I do play —as in *playing* poker—but it wasn't. It was work that required skill on many levels. Not only had I advanced in the rankings, I'd taken my winnings from $40,000, the amount Andros had given me to begin play minus my first night's loss, to $510,000, multiplying his investment by more than ten.

I wasn't only proud of my accomplishments on the poker table; I had information to share with Andros about Marion Elliott. There was nothing earth-shattering or surprising. Marion was a handsy old man who beamed when he discussed his favorite topic, himself.

Unzipping the side zipper on the black silk dress, I let it slide from my body revealing only the lace thong beneath. The way the silky material clung to my skin and the neckline plunged between my breasts, any additional undergarments would have been impossible to wear. After hanging the dress back in the closet, I entered the bathroom.

The emerald necklace hung heavily around my neck, out of place without more clothing. Unclasping it, I took it to the small safe and added it to the other treasures. After last night, I decided to add the recent night's chip receipt too.

Back into the bathroom, I stood in front of the mirror, turned away, and craned my neck. The sight of the small apple on my ass made me smile.

It was funny how I'd had the tattoo for over fifteen years and never had it brought me the pleasure it did last night. I didn't mean sexual gratification. I meant genuine happiness. If I closed my eyes, I recalled Patrick's expression as he came closer and ran his hand over the skin.

Wonder.

Awe.

Disbelief.

Pleasure.

Acknowledgment.

It all swirled in his blue eyes.

It was an experience I never expected to share. Now that I had, I knew Patrick was the only man, the only person, who would see the red fruit for what it truly meant.

While I would like the chance to talk to him once more, I was glad that earlier this afternoon I'd told him to stay away. I'd said it because I thought he'd stolen from me. That was no longer the case, but my current reasoning was direr. I couldn't take a chance of a visit with Andros near. Mitchell was gullible. Andros was not.

Patrick wouldn't understand the wrath of a man like Andros. I'd been wrong in presuming he'd stolen from me. Patrick was a good man, a man of morals. He shouldn't be exposed to a world like the Ivanov bratva. He deserved better.

My face was freshly washed and my hair combed out and tied back in a low ponytail when I slipped into my nightgown. Cotton with lace trim, it was the kind of sleeping attire I normally wore. I chose it for comfort, not appearance. With my untouchable status among the Ivanov men and my five-year agreement with Andros, nighttime meant sleep, not sex.

Allowing the exhaustion from the day to wash over me, I turned off the last light and climbed between the cool sheets. Slumber came swiftly.

I startled awake to the ringing of my phone. The dark room around me remained unchanged, yet my hands shook as if I'd been dreaming or perhaps having a nightmare. The phone rang again. I couldn't recall what I'd even been dreaming.

The screen of my phone said 1:32 a.m. One thing was for sure: I hadn't been asleep long. "Hello."

"My dear, your voice is a welcome sound," Andros said.

There was noise coming from behind his voice, other voices that I couldn't make out.

Was he at a club?

No, I didn't hear music, only voices.

"Are you busy?" I asked.

"It was I who called you. Mitchell tells me that you advanced."

I scooted up in the bed, sitting against the headboard with a smile. "I did. I did more than advance. My earnings have grown substantially."

"*My* earnings," he corrected.

"Yes, yours." I tried to regain my earlier enthusiasm. "It's a good thing. The more I have going into the final round, the better chances I have of winning. Your original investment has multiplied by more than twelve."

"Hmm."

His indifference caught me off guard. "That's over $500,000."

"I've never had trouble with math. The amount is inconsequential seeing as you could lose it tomorrow."

"I could. I won't. I played well, Andros. I thought—"

"You thought," he interrupted, "that you deserve praise for doing your job. That is like praising a dog for sitting or fetching a ball. The tasks aren't that difficult. I'm not dissatisfied with your play. Tell me about Marion Elliott."

Play.

It wasn't play.

I sighed. "I had a glass of wine with him before the tournament and learned that he'd ended the first night with $200,000."

"The first night?"

"Yes."

"Impressive. And your first night you didn't break even."

I swallowed the lump growing in my throat. "Yes, that's true. It was part of my strategy. Tonight I had over $500,000."

"And Elliott?"

"He didn't say specifically. He ended the night again in first place. From what I could deduce, his stack is tall. It might equal the jackpot."

"You spoke after the tournament?"

"Yes, I accepted his invitation to celebrate—as you'd told me to do." I added the last part to remind him that it was his doing.

"And you celebrated?"

"At Bar Regal. I'm certain Mitchell reported that too."

"Hmm. So tomorrow night you will bring me more than the million-dollar jackpot, additional millions or more in winnings."

My heartbeat thumped in my ears as the wine I'd consumed percolated in my stomach. "I'll do my best."

"I know you will. You will do your best because we both know that I don't like to be disappointed."

"Andros." The voices behind him were growing louder. "I should get to sleep."

"Did Elliott mention any of the other players? I heard there was another buy-in."

Patrick.

"When I spoke to Veronica this afternoon, yesterday," I

corrected, "the woman at Club Regal, she told me about the second buy-in."

"Before we saw one another?"

"Yes, I didn't think to mention it with all the talk of the handbag."

"My dear, I expect you to think."

Maybe I could if you weren't such a dick. "I'm sorry. Anyway, I'm telling you now. She told me that she wasn't in favor of either. The first one set a precedent making rejecting the second impossible."

"Interesting. And what was Elliott's opinion?"

I shook my head. "He didn't say much about that. His favorite subject was himself."

Andros's laugh came through the phone. "It's good that you've learned to be a good listener."

"It was all very mundane," I said, ignoring his continued disparaging comments. "Oil. Pipelines. Offshore drilling. He invited me to Texas, offering a tour of the oil fields." I mentioned the last part on purpose. While it was true, I guess I wanted Andros to know that Marion Elliott treated me better than he treated me. "He was very cordial."

"I don't need to ask for your reply to his invitation to drill."

Ugh. Of course, he'd think it was sexual. "You don't, but I respectfully declined."

"Did you give him your number?"

"No. I managed to change the subject."

"I doubt he will go to the trouble of tracking you down. However, even if he does, don't leave your room," he warned. "And keep the phone charged. I like the ability to keep track of my belongings. Currently your GPS has you where you belong."

Bile bubbled in my throat.

His belongings.

"Madeline, acknowledge that you heard and understand."

"I heard, Andros. I'm tired. I was asleep when you called. I have no intentions of leaving the room."

"There is work at hand that requires my full concentration. It's better if you're not a distraction."

I shook my head again. "I'm not. Good night." As I uttered the last syllable, the sound of the locking mechanisms echoed from my door.

My breath caught in my throat. "Is that you?"

"It is me saying good night, my dear. Stay put." The call went dead.

The door opened, coming to a stop at the engagement of the chain lock.

My skin cooled as I waited.

Should I scream?

Should I call the front desk?

"Madeline, open the door."

PATRICK

"*O*pen the chain," I demanded in a hushed growl, "or I'll fucking cut it."

"Patrick..." Madeline pleaded, her green-eyed stare coming from the small opening, "go away."

"Is he in there?"

Her head shook. "What? He? Who? There's no one here but me."

"Then open the goddamn door."

Without another word, her eyes closed and head tipped forward as the door closed.

With each passing second that I stood in the empty hallway my blood pressure rose.

Had she just locked me out?

I was ready to insert the key again and this time, kick in the damn door, freeing it from the chain, when the door clicked and opened inward. There she was—the calm to my racing pulse. Standing in a short cotton nightgown, her hair tied back in a low ponytail, and her face makeup free, was my Maddie. The lack of showmanship—the way she appeared at the tournament—stripped away the years until I could imagine us once again in the mission, two eighteen-year-old newlyweds who thought they were adults.

Simply put, she took my breath away.

I stepped inside the dark room. As the door swung shut, briefly the light from the hallway illuminated the entry. She was close enough to touch in a nightgown that came to above her knees, her arms, legs, and feet bare. Her complexion glistened, absolutely stunning.

Fuck. This was sexier than a negligee because this was real.

I fought the urge to smile.

First things first—I had a matter at hand that needed confirmation.

"Did he come back here with you?" I asked. "Did you have him meet you here after Mitchell brought you back?"

In the darkened space, her shadow moved until she twisted a switch, bringing soft golden illumination to the entry and room. Looking back at me, Madeline's head tilted and eyes narrowed. "What the hell, Patrick? Are you questioning me?"

My gaze went around the part of the room I could see. "Yes. Just tell me if he's here."

"Just tell you. To hell with you. I don't owe you an explanation for anything." Her neck straightened. "But you sure as shit do. Who the hell are you talking about? *He who?*"

I walked past her, taking in the expanse of the otherwise-empty room and the barely mussed bed. There were no signs of what had occurred the night before. The covers were hardly moved and only one pillow showed the sign of an indentation.

Without a word, I stalked back toward the entry and flung open the bathroom door. It bounced off the wall as I stepped inside. My shoes tapped upon the tile as I scanned each corner. With a huff, I pushed back the shower curtain.

Empty.

Determinedly, my steps found me back in the entry.

Madeline met me head-on. "What the actual fuck, Patrick? What is this with the macho-man act? Who are you looking to find?"

"Elliott," I said, unsure why she wouldn't know, seeing as they'd spent a good part of the night at Bar Regal together. "Where is he?"

Her chin snapped up. "If you must know, I have him tied up in the closet. And in other news, you're an asshole."

My gaze darted to the closed closet as I tried to make sense of her words. "You what?"

She pointed toward the door to the hallway. "Get out."

Undeterred, I reached for the handle to the closet door.

"If you open that," she proclaimed, "I never want to see you again."

Stepping away, I turned to her. "He's not here?"

"No, he's not. I don't know where he is. But even if he were here, it's none of your business. I hate to be the one to keep breaking this to you, but I'm not your concern."

Inhaling, I took a step back, spun slowly, and collected my breath as I ran my palm over the brittleness of my short hair. I'd tried to stay distanced, but watching her with Elliott had gotten to me. I hadn't even remembered to look for Ms. Standish. Madeline may say she wasn't my concern, yet the entire way here, the thought of her with Elliott consumed my thoughts.

When our gazes met again, I stared into her green orbs. "Madeline, I don't understand, why Marion Elliott?"

"Jeez, you're such a man." She slapped the sides of her thighs. "It has nothing to do with attraction."

"I saw you—watched you. You were smiling and laughing." I wanted that to be me, not him. I couldn't say that. Even in my head it sounded fucking pathetic.

Her head shook. "Like I said, I don't owe you an explanation." She sighed and sat at the edge of the bed. "I'll tell you the truth. My spending time with him was nothing more than research. I have to know my opponents. He landed the number-one spot two days in a row. Of course, I've heard of him. He asked me to have a drink last night. I refused. Tonight, I thought, okay, what can I learn?"

"Poker? That spectacle tonight was about poker?"

"Spectacle?"

"Probably not to anyone else."

"Whatever you want to call it. The answer is y-e-s." She drew out the word as she stood facing me. "Research. For your information, Marion Elliott is not my type."

"He's rich."

Her face spun back my way. "Thanks a lot, Patrick. You're saying I'm a gold digger? I'm a gambler and now a gold digger. Are there any more insults you'd like to hurl before I kick your ass out of my hotel room?"

"That's not...I didn't mean it that way. Some women find money attractive."

"So do men. Listen, I know how poor we were when we were young, but I've come to the conclusion that money doesn't buy happiness." She lifted her hand as I began to speak.

"Revolutionary, I know. I'm probably the first person in the history of mankind to realize that."

I scoffed. "Then I'm the second." I reached for her hand. "I'm sorry I assumed...that doesn't erase the fact that I fucking wanted to deck him—lay him out right there in Bar Regal."

She forced a laugh. "It doesn't work that way." Though I tried to speak, she continued, "Yes, there's a piece of paper somewhere that says two people, one who is no longer me, married. A piece of paper, that's all. I don't have any claims on you and you don't on me."

I did.

I had that paper.

I still had it.

And despite changing her name, she was still Madeline Tate who had married to become Madeline Kelly.

Instead of arguing, I reached forward and ran my finger over her warm cheek as I stared into her eyes. "You were stunning at the tournament, a fucking countess among peasants."

"Peasants? You weren't paying attention to their bets."

"I was," I said with a smile. "However, the bets weren't where I wanted my attention, or should I say on whom?" I cupped her chin and pulled her face toward mine. "They are all peasants compared to you. Not only are you strikingly gorgeous, you were amazing tonight. I checked the rankings and earnings before I left the club. Damn, you turned $40,000 into five hundred. That's pretty damn impressive."

Her smile bloomed. "Thank you. That's nice to hear."

"If that asshole didn't tell you how spectacular you were, I have another reason to deck him."

"Marion?" She shrugged. "He did say something, but it

sounds better coming from you." Stepping back, she reached for my hand. "I shouldn't have let you in. You shouldn't be here. Did anyone see you come in?"

"If you're worried about Leonardo, I waited until he left."

"Leonardo?" Madeline asked. "Oh, Mitchell. What do you mean left? This hallway?"

"The hotel."

"He left the hotel?" Her brow furrowed. "It doesn't matter. You still need to go." Her bare feet padded across the carpet as she went to the door and opened it. Taking a step forward, she peered one direction and then the other. Looking back over her shoulder she said, "The coast is clear. You can go now."

I reached for her hand and tugged her back into the room. "The coast is clear? Are we fifteen again?"

"Patrick, I mean it. You need to leave."

I pulled her closer. "Tell me that you want me to leave."

Maddie nodded. "I do."

I took a step back. "I'll leave, but you should know that now that I have confirmation that you're alive and so fucking amazing, I'm not giving up getting back and keeping who is mine."

"I'm not..."

"Piece of paper," I said.

"What you say isn't possible."

"And last night?"

Her hand came to my chest, her fingers splaying upon my starched shirt. "Last night was..." Pink blossomed like roses on her cheeks. "I will always remember it."

My hands skirted over her bare arms. "One more night, Maddie girl. Tell me you don't want that?"

"I can't."

My smile grew. "Good because it is just the beginning of what I want." I pulled my suit coat from my shoulders and tossed it onto a chair.

"No," she said. "You understood only part of what I meant. I *can't* tell you that I don't want you to stay because I do. I also *can't*. You do have to go. If Mitchell finds you here, I won't be able to explain."

"Does Leonardo come to your room in the middle of the night?"

She shook her head. "No, but..."

"Who does he report to?" The question just came to me. It didn't make sense that she would care so much about his opinion.

"What? No?" She exhaled. "That's not it. I have a reputation. Yes, I had drinks with Marion, but it wasn't a spectacle. I didn't go to his hotel or he to mine. I'm a woman in a male-dominated arena. If it would get out that you're here, every man would think he could sleep with me. I can't let that happen."

"If it got out, we could tell everyone the truth. I'm your husband."

Her head shook faster. "That can't get out either, for your sake and mine."

"I'm not leaving yet. We need to talk." When her worried expression remained, I added, "No one saw me and no one will see me."

Madeline exhaled. "How can you be sure?"

"I am." Unable to keep my distance, I seized her waist beneath the simple nightgown. The cloud of air surrounding her held the faint aroma of soap and toothpaste. Splaying my fingers,

I pulled her closer until her warmth came to my chest and her small hands to my shoulders. My palms skirted over her sides, upward to the swell of her breasts, and down to the curvature of her hips.

"Pa-trick."

The way she elongated my name was Viagra to my dick.

I wanted to talk, we needed to. Yet with her against me, there was a more pressing matter, one that had grown and developed in record time having her in my grasp. "I want you, Maddie girl."

She peered up. "That name is so juvenile."

"We can be one hundred years old, and I'll still see you as my Maddie girl. I am going to kiss you."

Sexier than the purr of the heat through the ducts, her soft hum reverberated through the air, bringing warmth to everything it reached. I cupped her cheeks, bringing her lips to mine, tasting what I had only inhaled.

Sparks ignited.

Fire and mint.

Together we moved closer, taking as well as giving. Her arms encircled my neck as my grip tightened. Our tongues danced in sync, delving, as our lips unapologetically bruised one another, and the room filled with the songs of pleasure.

Reaching for the hem of her nightgown, I lifted it upward.

Madeline stopped me. "That's not talking. I don't know when we'll have another chance to talk. You said you wanted to talk."

"I'm going to make love to my wife first, and then once we're both satisfied, we will talk."

Her eyes opened wide. "That didn't sound like a question."

This time, I lifted the gown.

Her body was now only covered by a slight triangle of black lace. As my gaze moved upward, I took in her round tits, darkening areolas, and tightening nipples. My hiss filled the air. When our eyes finally met, hers were a molten green, swirling with what I hoped was desire.

"It wasn't a question," I said, reaching for her hand, "but that doesn't mean you can't say no."

"No."

We both stilled as I repeated the one-syllable word. "No."

"No, I don't want to say that. I want you, too."

In one swoop, I lifted her from the ground. Carrying her to where the bedcovers were folded back, I lowered her to the sheet. Taking hold of the tie in her hair, I gently pulled it free, unleashing her long ebony locks. "You're so damn beautiful."

"You make me feel that way."

"It's the way you should feel every damn day."

Her melancholy smile twisted a knife I didn't understand and couldn't identify. "Maddie, talk to me."

Her head shook. "Not yet. Do what you said you were going to do."

Make love to my wife.

My grin grew as I released my cufflinks, placing them in my pants pocket, unbuttoned my shirt, removed it from my shoulders, and tossed it to the floor. Preceded by my shoes, my belt and trousers followed. Though my boxer briefs were still in place, my erection was growing painful, and pressing against the silk, it was hard to miss.

"You've become a handsome man," Madeline said, her eyes wide as she took me in.

"You have always been the most beautiful woman even when you were still a girl." I reached for the waistband of her tiny excuse for panties. She wiggled, allowing me to slide them down her thighs, calves, and over her painted toenails until they joined our other clothes littering the carpeting.

"Oh..." she whimpered as my tongue found her core.

She was a fucking luscious apple that I wanted to eat, lick by lick and nip by nip until the juice coated my tongue and chin. Her hips bucked and fingers splayed over my hair as her sounds of pleasure grew louder. It was as I sucked her clit that the earthquake within her began.

Pushing down my boxers, I climbed over her sensuous body, the curves of her hips, flat plane of her stomach, and softness of her tits, as her legs spread wider, allowing me access. With my erection poised at her entrance, I stopped.

"Maddie, open your eyes. See me." It was a glimpse at heaven that met me as her lids blinked open. "No one else can hear you say it. You can deny it until the day I die, but just this once, let me hear you say your name."

She wiggled beneath me. "Please, I'm so ready."

"Who...tell me...who is ready?"

MADELINE

I was lost, floating in a sea of blue, as I stared up at the sincerity in Patrick's eyes.

Adrift in a world of long ago, in a time when two lost souls, embodied in the beings of two petty thieves, found the honesty that comes with adolescent love. Without the constraints and responsibilities of age, the love we shared was all that we needed. Food, shelter, and even safety paled in comparison. Our mutual affection wrapped us in a warm cocoon at night and heated our days with desire. Together we were unstoppable until...

My eyes closed as his image blurred.

"Let me see."

Swallowing the emotion of our destruction, I did as he said and again opened my eyes. This time Patrick's thumb wiped away a tear I hadn't known had fallen.

"Push them away," he said.

It was what he'd said the night before. I didn't want to push the thoughts away. I wanted to go back in time, to build a time machine and linger in that era of lost innocence.

Patrick's lips peppered my cheeks with kisses. "I won't push you. Say it when you mean it."

Palming his bristly cheeks, I pushed his head away until I could see all of his handsome face. Protruding brow, satin blue eyes with lashes too long to be a man's, high cheekbones, and a defined, chiseled jaw appeared before me. "I can't. I know it's not exactly what you want to hear, but I will admit that I like to hear it from you even if it sounds juvenile."

Patrick's smile curled upward. "My Maddie."

I nodded.

It wasn't what he wanted to hear, but it worked. My back arched and I cried out as for one last time, our two lost souls became one. Though my core fought the invasion, my mind wanted more. I wiggled and lifted my hips to accommodate him.

It had been too long since I'd made love, probably seventeen years. Over the last five years, any kind of sex had been nonexistent—that was until last night. And now, two nights in a row, my muscles protested as together we found our rhythm.

This wasn't rushed or erratic.

Slow and thorough, Patrick moved. This was what it was like to make love.

Kisses, praises, and caresses overwhelmed me.

Patrick worshipped everything about me as he encouraged my climb. Higher and higher. No longer taut from underuse but from the rush of desire, every nerve and muscle within me was on the brink of explosion. Clawing at his broad shoulders, I clung to him as time after time, he made my world implode.

When I thought it wasn't possible to get there again, he'd

find a way. It was as he'd always been, the one who persisted and prevailed. The one who refused to let the two of us become lost to the streets. Patrick was still that same person, pushing me—no, encouraging me.

It wasn't only me who found release. His neck would strain and the air filled with his guttural roar, and yet we weren't done. We began the dance again.

Perhaps we both knew this was the last time. Such as riding a roller coaster that both excites and thrills, neither of us was ready to get off.

I wouldn't allow myself to think about the consequence were our reunion discovered.

The ride would be closed, quite possibly the entire park. Andros didn't play fair nor did he share. I couldn't think about it. Instead I chose to take what I could of Patrick, giving in return, and hope the memories would last me the remainder of my lifetime.

The face of my phone read after three thirty in the morning when Patrick left me to enter the bathroom only to return with a warm washcloth. There was something about the tenderness with which he tended to me that brought the lump back to my throat. "I don't recall you doing this before?" I said, searching my memories. "It seems oddly intimate."

Such a peculiar thought after all the pleasure we'd brought one another, and yet it was true. Having him gently clean me was personal and private in a way sex was not.

Patrick's grin spread across his face. "Even at the mission, we had to leave our room and go into the hall for running water."

The small room he was talking about appeared in my memory. Smaller than this hotel room with a communal shared bathroom, it had been the closest to a real home we'd shared. We'd been allowed to move in after we could prove our marriage.

Before that, it had been abandoned buildings, underpasses, tents, and of course, his carved-away room hidden behind a wall.

Taking the washcloth back to the bathroom, Patrick returned to the bed. "I know it's late. I should let you sleep. But, Maddie girl, I need answers and I believe I have a plan."

"Stay a little longer," I consented, unwilling to lose what we were sharing.

Patrick might have questions, but I knew that I couldn't tell him what he deserved to hear. However, his talk of a plan had me intrigued.

The bed dipped as Patrick settled his naked body beside mine, his head on the pillow as his long legs stretched under the covers. I lifted my head to his strong shoulder and mindlessly ran the tips of my fingers over his defined chest and abdomen. It was difficult for my mind to fathom the way he'd matured and the man he'd become. "Patrick, it makes me sad to think of you being alone. You should find someone."

His arm around my shoulder tightened. "I did."

I lifted my head. "This isn't real. Soon I'll be gone."

"I have a plan that will work."

"You do?" I asked with a grin. "It's just like you to think you can fix things that are unfixable."

He reached toward me and smoothed a rogue strand of hair away from my face. "I told you that I checked the results before I left the club."

"Yes."

"Five hundred and ten thousand dollars is a lot of money."

"I suppose." Terms such as 'a lot' and 'a little' were too subjective to argue.

"Take it."

"What?" I asked, trying to make sense of what he was saying. "I can't *take it*. I need it to make my bets. I need it to advance from the next round and win the final."

His eyes closed as he shook his head. "I'm being as honest as I can. I can't say too much..." He inhaled. "You are not going to win. You can't. But if you listen to me now, you can walk away with half a million dollars."

I pulled away from his hold and with a huff, flopped back on the neighboring pillow. Reaching for the sheets and blankets, I pulled them up over my breasts. "You don't think I can do it."

Patrick followed, the warmth of his chest lingering over me as he looked down into my eyes. "That wasn't what I said. I know you can. I also know it won't happen. Maddie, you're here to play a tournament. There is more happening. The tournament is nothing more than the battlefield. I don't want you to be a casualty. I won't let that happen. If this tournament goes too far, you could be left with nothing."

I swallowed, thinking of Andros's decree. "That can't happen."

"Then cash out," he said, as if it were that easy. "Take the money and then you can stay here in Chicago."

"If that were possible, which it's not, tell me what would happen next. Tell me where you see me fitting into this plan."

"I'll get you an apartment or better yet a house." His tone lightened. "Remember when we used to talk about the suburbs and a yard?"

My lips pursed. "You'll get me...you'll supply this mythical house with a yard and a picket fence. At that point, what will I be? Maybe your mistress, the woman you keep hidden?"

He ran his finger over my cheek. "No, Madeline. You'll be what you are, my wife, and all I want to hide you from is the cruelty that occurs in this city. I can keep you safe."

"Safety is an illusion, Patrick."

"I can't tell you how, but I can do it. I know I can."

His sincerity made me scoff. Pushing his hand away, I threw back the covers and stood, naked and honest before him. This couldn't go on. "It is late," I said. "I need sleep because I don't have a choice. I must win. I can't say more either, nor will I, but the consequence of my not winning is too monumental for it to be a possibility." Looking around the floor, I found my nightgown. After I'd pulled it over my head, I smiled. "Thank you."

"What in the hell are you thanking me for?" He too stood and began collecting his clothes. "I offered you a solution, but you sound like you won't take it."

"I'm thanking you for tonight and last night. I can't take your offer, but know I won't forget you." *I never have.*

His boxers were in place and his trousers were pulled up, yet his wide chest was bare. "We still haven't talked. I deserve at least one answer."

I pulled the lace thong up my legs and back into place before smoothing the nightgown. Looking back up, our gazes met. "I'm not sure if I can give it." My chin came up. "But go ahead, ask."

He reached for my arms. "What happened? Why did you disappear?"

I closed my eyes. Memories came and went in a whirlwind of chaos.

Fear.

Anguish.

Terror.

Even joy.

It was all a lifetime ago.

Andros's dead stare came to mind.

I'd made a deal with the devil, and given the same circumstances, I'd do it again.

When my eyes opened, Patrick was staring down at me. "I was eighteen. Things happen when you're eighteen."

His neck straightened. "What kind of things?"

"Things that go beyond our control. All that matters now is that we both..." I forced a smile. "...made it to the other side." It wasn't all that mattered, but it was all I would say.

Pushing myself up on my tiptoes, I gave him a chaste kiss. "That goes for you too. Your clothes..." I picked up his suit coat, feeling the luxurious wool blend and handed it to him. "...are expensive. I've watched you. You're betting hundreds of thousands of dollars in the tournament. Think about where we were. There shouldn't be any sadness. In reality, we should congratulate ourselves. We made it."

"Remember what you said about money and happiness?" he asked as he shrugged his suit coat over his broad shoulders.

The two don't equate.

I nodded.

"I'd trade it all to hold you every night."

I smiled. "You're too kind. Sometimes what we want isn't just out of reach, it's too far gone." I took a quick glance toward the windows, and while the drapes were closed, I remembered the time of year, thankful that it was January, and the sun would still be below the horizon. "Please go. I need sleep."

After buttoning his suit coat, Patrick removed his phone from the pocket and his expression grimaced.

"Is everything all right?"

"It seems I've missed a few things." He shoved the phone back in the pocket. "Madeline, I can't let you go. Say you'll stay...at least until Sunday."

"I don't know. It's not up to me."

"Your driver, or whatever he is, determines your schedule? Or is it someone else?"

I couldn't tell him about Andros.

That information would be his death sentence.

There was power that surrounded Patrick. However, it was calm and strong, demanding yet accommodating. He was a giant sequoia, strong and regal, bending to the winds yet not broken. Andros was a devastating tornado or a wildfire, capable of destroying what had been unharmed for thousands of years.

I wouldn't let their paths cross. Patrick wouldn't understand the brutality of the Ivanov bratva.

I'd rather die of a broken heart, again, than bring any real harm to my first love.

"Bye, Patrick. Please stay safe." Because you sure as hell don't need to be pulled into my world—you wouldn't survive.

He reached for the doorknob. "This is fucking harder than it was when you were asleep."

I nodded as tears came to my eyes. "Wait, let me check the hallway." I pushed past him and peered into the corridor. Apparently, after four on a Saturday morning, the hallway was still empty.

"Is the coast clear?" he asked.

I nodded, swallowing my sorrow. That did sound like a teenage phrase. "Goodbye. I beg you not to acknowledge knowing me at the tournament, not more than simply as an opponent."

He kissed the top of my head. "I'll pretend if that's what you want, but know I'm thinking about how it feels to be inside you and the way you moan as I'm going down on you."

"Patrick."

"That's not all."

"It is," I said. "You need to go."

"You can pretend too, but tell me what you'll be thinking when you see me?"

That you're the only man I ever loved. I didn't say that. "I'll be concentrating on the cards because I must win. Please...goodbye."

Patrick also looked both directions before slipping into the hallway. Wrapping my arms around myself, I collapsed against the door, holding back the tears. Shakily, I reached for the chain and secured the door. Turning off the light, I fell into the soft bed, surrounded by his scent.

Staring at the ceiling, I berated myself for agreeing to this tournament, for allowing Andros to bully me into attending. Up until now, I'd successfully avoided Chicago. I'd made excuses, never divulging the real reason.

Now that I was here, I realized that I avoided the city because I didn't want to know Patrick's fate. I didn't want to learn that he had died or maybe even married again.

"I'm sorry, Patrick."

Tears fell to the pillow as I finally gave in to slumber.

PATRICK

*T*here was no avoiding the other Sparrows. From the litany of text messages, they had news, and I'd spent the last two hours unreachable. After parking the car in our private garage, I entered the elevator. Even my presence in the garage would set off alarms. If Sparrow, Reid, and Mason were on two, they now knew where I was.

Inhaling, I straightened my suit coat for the one hundredth time. Even before I could hit the button, the elevator arrived. As I entered, the light for two was lit. That meant they'd sent it for me and preprogrammed it to stop at two.

Fuck.

This was an unavoidable command performance. It wasn't unique and didn't necessarily have a negative connotation. It was what we did to one another when the other's presence was wanted or needed. From the command center the elevator could be rerouted. It had been. I sucked in a breath as the elevator began to move ninety-plus stories into the sky.

I made up my mind. I'd tell them about Madeline.

I would.

I'd go back to the beginning and tell them what happened seventeen years ago...forget that, twenty years ago, the day I pulled her into the room in the wall, when she offered to share her bounty of apples with me. When out of the whole crazy fucking world, in the middle of mayhem and survival, a girl pretending to be a boy made my life suddenly worth living.

I would tell them the truth.

I hadn't hidden the information. There had been no reason to divulge it.

She disappeared.

In the world we lived in, disappearance usually ultimately resulted in death.

Seventeen years had passed without a word until Thursday night.

Yes.

I stood straighter as I went higher. It was decided. That was what I'd tell them and they'd understand. I presumed it wouldn't be an easy conversation, but we'd had those before. The memory of a more recent discussion came back to me. It occurred after Mason called our secure covert number. There had been shock, disbelief, and confusion, yet we survived, stronger as a team.

I swallowed. This would be all right.

I would explain that since Thursday night my attention had been diverted, not by some subversive plot to overtake Chicago, but by man's oldest distraction. Like Adam had been distracted by Eve, Madeline was my forbidden fruit.

Apple.

Wait. No.

Eve brought about the downfall of man with one bite of an apple.

Bad example.

I needed to think of a better illustration.

Bathsheba?

I wasn't certain why biblical examples were the ones coming to mind.

The elevator stopped. My time was up.

The doors opened to the concrete corridor on two. With another deep breath, I laid my palm over the sensor. The metal door immediately moved sideways. Our command center was in front of me, full of activity. Some of the screens over our heads were moving from one view to the next, bringing the mostly sleeping city of Chicago in bits and pieces before our eyes.

I stood within the room as the door shut behind me, looking at the large screens over where Reid was working. I recognized every one of the eighteen faces. One was mine. Three had been sitting at the same table as I had during the tournament. The other fourteen included Antonio Hillman, Marion Elliott, and Madeline Kelly. No, the name beside her picture read Madeline Miller.

From where I stood I could see Mason's face, but not what he was doing, and then there was Sparrow lying on his back, his feet planted on the ground and his spine straight on top of a weight bench. It wasn't unusual for one of us to pump iron or run on one of the treadmills as we worked and brainstormed. What was unusual was for someone to be holding a bar with weights the size of the ones on Sparrow's bar without a spotter.

The long bar bowed with the weight as it hovered above his chest.

Throwing off my suit coat, I hurried to stand near Sparrow's head. "How about a spotter?" I asked as I read the black discs. Two one-hundred-pound plates were at each end.

That wasn't a good sign.

It meant he was frustrated or angry. I'd been around these men too long to not know their tells.

Sparrow's biceps trembled, the muscles quivering below his t-shirt sleeve as he lowered the weight and after readjusting his grip, pushed higher, locking his elbows. His count was audible as I fought the need to look back up at Madeline's picture. I couldn't.

I waited.

"8, 7, 6, 5, 4, 3, 2, 1."

I reached for the bar and lifted it to the cradle above Sparrow's head. When our eyes met, I asked, "What have I missed?"

Sitting upward, Sparrow wiped the perspiration from his brow with the tail of his t-shirt and after snatching a bottle of water that had been near his feet and taking a long draw, he exhaled. "Where have you been?"

"I was checking out a lead." I looked up at the screens. All the high-end hotel entrances and exits rotated across the feed. I couldn't lie. There was a chance I'd been seen. "...At the Palmer House."

Sparrow nodded. Standing, he patted my shoulder. "Good job in the tournament." His smile grew. "Best fucking news all day, and it's been shitty, but the idea of you turning a hundred grand into three hundred plus some change in a few hours was the bright spot."

I tried to smile. "Okay, I won. I'll keep winning. Tell me what's been shitty?"

Mason lifted his head from the far side of the computer banks. "Hillman went to McIver's."

"That's good. Isn't it? It's what we expected."

"It is and it isn't. He didn't stay long," Mason said, "and neither did his entourage. I think it was a distraction. They hoped we'd stop watching. We didn't. Each person took a separate vehicle, ones they had waiting parked near McIver's."

"What?" I said. "They had vehicles waiting at McIver's? The parking there is shit."

"Which means," Sparrow chimed in, "someone allowed it. I fucking hate that club. I want you..." He was speaking to Mason. "...to go there first thing in the morning and find out who authorized the parking or even whose vehicles they were."

"I can do it," I volunteered.

His dark eyes came my way. "You have a tournament to win. I want you to sleep."

"No. They know me..." I hated bringing up that Mason had been gone, but sometimes even he needed the reminder. "...they're used to me," I rephrased.

"Did my order sound like it was up for debate to anyone else?" Sparrow asked unnecessarily loud.

When no one responded, I looked back up at the screens. "You're right. I need some sleep. First, do you know where Hillman and his men went?"

"It took a while. They went all around the city, stopping at several of the hotels and picking up a few riders," Reid said.

"One," Mason added, "picked up a man at the Palmer. He looked familiar. I think he was at Club Regal last night."

My gut twisted. "Do you have a picture?"

"Yeah, give me a few."

"If someone at McIver's had tipped us off..." Reid began.

"...wanted to keep their fucking doors open," Sparrow rephrased.

"...we could have put trackers on the cars."

"Okay," I said, "we didn't have trackers, but man, Reid, you found them. I know you did. Where did they go?"

"Abandoned house in Jefferson Park," Reid replied. "I've been working on traffic cams. Problem is that the neighborhood where they were is so shitty even the cameras don't all work. Kids think it's fun to shoot them out as soon as a new one is placed." He continued typing. "I've been working for hours. Honestly, it's a fucking great location for avoiding surveillance."

"As if they know," I said.

"Hillman would," Reid said. "However, we don't think it was only Hillman and his men. The pictures from the feed are grainy and the lighting sucks. Anyway, besides the people Hillman's men picked up, there were more, about another four cars. Apparently, there was a party we weren't invited to attend."

He pulled up a shot of the street. It was as he said, dark and grainy. Cars could be seen parked along the curbs, cars nicer than you'd normally see in an area like this.

"How about license plates?" I asked.

"Rental companies," Reid went on. "Mason has been trying to access the agreements, but we've been spread pretty thin."

"Sorry," I muttered.

"Did your lead pay off?" Sparrow asked.

No. She said she's leaving the city and won't tell me where she will go.

"Not really. I should have been here."

"You need to go with your gut," Mason said. "It may not always be right, but it's rarely wrong. You're here now. I could use a hand with the rental agreements so I can go back to running facial recognition software on a few of our better shots."

"I've been running background checks on your opponents," Reid said.

"And I've been meeting with capos on one," Sparrow volunteered. "The reports are coming in, but everything is scattered. There have been some blowups with a few different gangs. It's bullshit stuff that shouldn't be an issue. I could see if it were summer, but fuck, it's like ten degrees out there. Why cause problems now?"

Summer nights, when the temperatures were sweltering, it wasn't uncommon to have an increase in violence and gang activity. It wasn't a phenomenon limited to Chicago. Even smaller cities like Gary, Detroit, Indianapolis, Cleveland, and St. Louis noticed it.

I pulled out one of the chairs and spun it around, straddling the back as I rolled the sleeves of my shirt to my elbows.

"No cufflinks?" Mason asked.

"Yeah, they're in my pocket. I was preparing to go to sleep before the elevator brought me to all your shining faces." I logged onto the program they'd already set up with the license plates and rental car companies and began searching the money trail.

"Here's the man picked up at the Palmer House," Reid said.

I looked up at the screen.

Shit.

"He was at the tournament," Mason said. "I know I saw

him."

My stomach twisted. "His name is Mitchell Leonardo."

"How do you know that?" Mason asked.

"He has been at the tournament," I said. "He gave me an odd feeling."

"Do you know more?" Sparrow asked.

My head shook. "I wish I did. All I know is that he's here for the tournament, watching, not playing."

"If he's here for the tournament, why did he attend Hillman's house party tonight?" Mason asked.

Reid began typing. "It fucking helps when I have a name."

"So this," Sparrow began, "nobody who is attending Club Regal's poker tournament isn't a player?"

"No," I said. "He mentioned he preferred the ponies. I sat near him at the bar trying to get a read on him. He told me that he's just passing through."

Sparrow nodded. "For a poker tournament? I agree, it feels off."

"It might not be that far off," Mason said. He pointed up to the screen. "See the woman?"

My stomach dropped. If something Mitchell Leonardo was involved in implicated Madeline, I was paying him a visit before the next round.

The men were talking. "...see here," Reid said. "I can find multiple instances of him leaving or arriving at the Palmer House with Ms. Miller. They're always in a taxi cab."

"What do we know about her?" Sparrow asked.

"Do you think we should worry about her when Hillman is having house parties in some of the worst places in the city?" I asked.

"You don't?" Mason asked. "They're connected."

Exhaling, I leaned forward on the seat's back and resumed my research of rental cars. "Of course, everyone is suspect."

"Her background is pretty boring," Reid said. "Wikipedia has a cute little bio. Daughter of average parents, average town, parents deceased, never married, yada, yada."

"Then why does she need a goon?" Mason asked.

"What about Hillman? Is he back from his house party?" I asked.

"Yes, he and his entire entourage," Reid answered. "They're all back at the Four Seasons. I saw them all enter Hillman's suite."

"Has the goon guy returned to the Palmer House?" I asked.

"Not yet," Mason said.

Sparrow began to pace. "We fucking need sleep. Is Elliott back at his hotel?"

"Yes," Reid said, "he's been back since he left the club."

"I'm coming up blank," I said. "The cars were rented by three different LLCs from five different rental companies."

"Yeah, I was hoping you'd find something different," Mason said.

"Credit cards go to the same LLCs."

"Let me guess," Sparrow said, "all from the same state."

"Delaware," I said, knowing that setting up a shell company in Delaware was one of the easiest, as easy as an email account, and could be done in one day.

"Patrick, go get some sleep," Sparrow said. "This isn't a debate. You and Mason both came to the same dead end. I think we can safely assume that whoever rented those cars doesn't want to be identified."

"Hillman is parading around Chicago's finest private clubs. He's not hiding."

"Check his reservation at the Four Seasons," I said. "It's in his name. Is it booked with his own credit card? Who knows, this could go back to McFadden money. We all know there's a shit ton out there that the feds haven't been able to find. McFadden has it hidden away."

"Patrick, I fucking mean it," Sparrow said. "You can't count cards and beat Hillman without some sleep. He's not leaving my city with millions in his pocket to fund some kind of coup. What time does the first round begin tomorrow?" He scoffed. "Today?"

"Noon," I said as I stood. "First, I need to mention something."

The entire room stopped, all eyes turned my way.

"You sick?" Reid asked.

"No."

"Will it affect tomorrow?" Sparrow asked. "Will it make a difference with Hillman and McFadden's men coming back to town? Because we need to be razor focused. Other shit can wait."

"I don't believe it will," I answered.

"Then go to bed," Sparrow proclaimed.

Nodding, I started to walk toward the steel door. Before reaching it, I turned back around. "Tomorrow is the big night at the club. I think we should all get some shut-eye. The capos will notify us if things get out of control."

"He's right," Sparrow said. "You two," he spoke to Mason and Reid, "let the programs run. Get some sleep. We're not all winning a poker tournament tomorrow, but we may be needed."

PATRICK

Three hours' sleep wasn't much, but it would have to be enough. By the time I showered, dressed, and made my way up to the penthouse kitchen, the room was full.

"Good morning," Araneae, Sparrow's wife, said with a smile over her coffee mug.

"Is my calendar wrong?" I asked. "What is everyone doing up on a cold Saturday morning? Hell, I'd sleep in if I could."

Reid's wife, Lorna, who was standing at the stove top flipping bacon and filling the room with an amazing aroma, laughed. "Patrick, when was the last time you slept in?"

"Probably," Reid said, "before they busted our asses in basic training."

A small smile came to my lips, imagining that time—before I joined the service, before Maddie disappeared. The image of the two of us cuddled under a thick blanket brought warmth to my face. When I snapped out of it, all eyes were on me. "I guess you're right. I was just thinking how nice it would be."

"Grab some coffee," Sparrow said, "and explain the tournament. I'm thinking of joining you for the final round."

"No," came the resounding call from Mason, Reid, and me.

"Why? What's happening?" Araneae asked as she sat beside Sparrow.

"Nothing," Sparrow said as he flashed her a grin.

"Yeah, I don't believe you," she said. And then she turned to me. "Come on, Patrick, you're supposed to do what I say. What's happening and why can't Sterling be there?"

Sparrow had once told me that—to listen to her—and even though she was saying it in jest, it was something she liked to remind me of. "I'm playing cards," I answered honestly.

"Cards?" all three women echoed.

"Poker," Mason clarified. "It's a tournament with a million-dollar jackpot on top of substantial earnings. Patrick has made it to the semifinals. Tonight is the final."

"Is this legal?" Araneae asked.

"What if you don't win in the semi-finals?" Laurel, Mason's wife, asked.

"Yes," Sparrow answered his wife and turning to Laurel, he said, "That won't happen."

"Poker sounds fun," Lorna said. "I say we have a house poker party one of these cold nights instead of you four working away downstairs."

"And we'll have wine," Araneae added.

"And snacks," Lorna replied as she lifted a platter of bacon onto the table.

Laurel stood and brought over a bowl of fruit.

From the oven, Lorna added a large bowl of scrambled eggs and added it to the center. Before long, we were all feasting on the morning's spread while I explained the workings of the Club Regal tournament. "Eighteen players will begin the early round today. Depending upon the betting, eighteen may not complete it."

"Why?" Laurel asked.

"Have you ever played poker?" Mason asked her with a grin. "I mean, I would be happy to teach you."

Pink filled her cheeks. "Why am I thinking strip poker?"

"Because that was what I was thinking," he said.

"I can teach you," Araneae volunteered with a smirk. "And then you can still play strip poker, but you'll be the one with the view."

Sparrow cleared his throat.

His wife laughed. "Sure, I'll take you on. You'll lose too, but Laurel's view is more—"

"More what?" Sparrow asked.

Everyone's meal was momentarily forgotten as we waited, wondering how Araneae was going to ease her way out of this conversation corner.

Araneae's head tilted. "More colorful. Mine, though, will be the best."

The room filled with laughter. It was an alternate universe within the homes of our glass castle, a strange reality where our family, though not by blood, could live and love despite the dangers lurking within our city. It was comforting and sad. For only a moment my thoughts went to Madeline. I could make her safe, just as these men had done for their women.

I pushed the thought away. It was not the way a man like me lived, and with Maddie's constant denials, it wouldn't happen. I needed to concentrate on what I could do.

"As I was saying," I began after another sip of coffee. "All-in wasn't an option in the first two rounds. It is now. It's the best way to eliminate opponents."

"Risky," Sparrow said.

"Not to be done in a bluff. Not usually," I said.

"So if all eighteen players end the round with chips, who advances?" Laurel asked, seeming genuinely curious.

"The six players who have accumulated the most during the round."

"Not overall winnings?" Lorna asked.

"No, those are the house rules. The rationale being that overall wouldn't be fair. The top forty-two buy-ins entered the tournament. The money was uneven from the start. Entering with more capital is enough advantage without adding that to daily winnings.

"Now, I am beginning the round with around $300,000. I'd venture to guess the person sitting at number one has in excess of a million." My assumption was based on Madeline's $500,000 in eighth place. "The money you begin play with is deducted to assess your placement. Top six advance."

Laurel's head was shaking. "The more money you begin with the better your chances would seem."

I nodded. "It's true, but then again, the all-in option can flip the winnings very fast."

"That's a lot of money," Araneae said.

Laurel continued her questions. "And if you win it all—the whole tournament—"

"When," Sparrow interjected.

"*When* you win it all," Laurel said with a grin, "do you get to only win the jackpot or do you keep your chips as well?"

"The winner keeps both." I thought about it for a second. It's smart of a tournament to be run this way. If the players couldn't keep their earnings, they would be more frivolous with their bets. "Even if the player doesn't win the jackpot, if they never lose an all-in, that person could leave the tournament with a fair amount of cash."

My phone vibrated in my pocket.

"Excuse me." I pulled my phone from my pocket and read the text message. "It's from Beckman," I said for the benefit of the other men.

"I NEED TO SPEAK TO YOU RIGHT AWAY. IS NOW A GOOD TIME?"

I stood. "He wants to talk."

"You're not backing out of the tournament, no matter what pressure he's under," Sparrow said. "My city. If he plans on keeping that club open..."

I nodded as I walked into the large living room. It was not far from the kitchen, yet far enough to keep my conversation away from the women. And as I paused, it sounded as if their conversation had resumed.

Similar to all of our individual apartments, this floor of Sparrow and Araneae's penthouse had floor-to-ceiling windows. I looked outside at the lake and city below. Even on this cold morning, the sun was rising, breaking through the morning frost and haze.

My city.

Sparrow's proclamation rang in my ears. It was his and ours. We'd worked to secure it and allowing Hillman, one of McFadden's old guard, to come in here and showboat, sling insults, and walk away with millions of dollars wouldn't—couldn't—be allowed.

Hitting the icon near Ethan Beckman's name, I waited for the call to connect. "Beckman?" I asked after he answered.

"Mr. Kelly, there's so much blood. I-I don't...she's dead."

Turning back toward the archway to the kitchen, I caught the three sets of eyes looking my direction. Reid, Mason, and Sparrow were no longer in the kitchen but standing shoulder to shoulder, staring at me in anticipation.

My knees felt weak as the room around me spun.

Madeline?

Dead?

How would Beckman know to call me?

Why did I leave her?

My pulse raced as questions fought for supremacy. "Wait. How did you know to call me?"

"I-I figured you could get a message to Mr. Sparrow. I didn't know what else to do."

"To Mr. Sparrow?" I looked across the room as my mind tried to make sense of what Beckman was saying. "Yes, I can. Tell me what you want me to relay."

His voice cracked as he spoke faster. "The thing is, she's always here early, especially when there's an event."

"Wait. Who is always there early?"

"Veronica Standish."

Exhaling, I leaned against the back of one of the many sofas. "Veronica Standish."

"Yes, sir. You were speaking to her last evening. She's almost always here..."

"Yes, I know who she is."

"She doesn't live far from Club Regal," Beckman said.

"Ms. Standish," I said one more time for confirmation.

"Yes, sir. When she didn't answer her phone, I presumed she'd overslept. There are too many things that need to be done before the tournament at noon. I will admit, I was angry that she wasn't here. We'd had a series of disagreements about this tournament."

"How do you know that she's dead?"

"After a few calls, I decided to go over to her place myself. It's awful. I've never seen—"

"Calm down. You found her?" My head was shaking. "Have you called the police?"

"Not yet. I'm here...I didn't know what to do. I-I...please; I just thought Mr. Sparrow would want to know. That's why I called you first."

"Mr. Beckman, take a deep breath. Let me inform Mr. Sparrow." I didn't wait for a response before hitting the mute button on the phone. I then relayed what I'd just heard, speaking softly so as to not alarm the women.

"Tell him to wait for our forensics team," Sparrow said. "Once they arrive he's to go to the club and go on like a normal day. Not a word to anyone else."

I nodded.

"Tell him," Sparrow went on, "that he'll be rewarded for his loyalty for calling you first. After our people get a look at the scene, the police can be notified anonymously."

I unmuted the phone. "Stay where you are."

"Here?" he asked. "No, sir, I can't...I mean, what if someone assumes—"

"Stop, Ethan," I said calmly. "You did the right thing calling me first. Mr. Sparrow is pleased with your order of actions. Stay put until our team arrives. Tell me it wasn't you and you won't be implicated."

"It wasn't, Mr. Kelly, I swear. Oh God. The blood."

"Don't touch anything. Whatever you have already touched, tell our team. After they arrive, go back to the club and act like it's a normal day."

"I-I...don't know that I can."

"Don't disappoint Mr. Sparrow, Beckman. You can do this. We need to learn the details and find out who did this. I'll leave right away. The team will be there soon." I looked over at Reid who was sending what I believed was the message to the capo in charge of these jobs. He looked up from his phone and nodded. "Yes, they've been notified. I'll meet you back at the club. Tell me you can do this."

"I-I..."

"Tell me we can count on you," I said again.

"Yes...yes, I can stay. You can count on me. What about the police?" he asked.

"Once our team has learned all they can, the police will receive an anonymous call. Don't call anyone else."

"Yes, sir. I was upset with her, but I never wanted..."

"Of course you didn't. Stay put until the team arrives."

I disconnected the line.

"Why?" Sparrow asked. "Veronica Standish has been a staple..." He did a full turn as his fingers raked through his hair. "Tell me everything he said."

I nodded and turned to Reid to confirm what we'd silently said. "The team on its way?"

"Yes. Marcelo replied. They're good."

"All right. Can you confirm that I was Beckman's first call and his last until this is resolved?"

"I'm going with you," Sparrow said. "You can fill me in on the way."

My jaw clenched. "Boss, it's your call. I would prefer if you didn't, at least not yet."

"I'll go with Patrick," Mason volunteered. "I was going anyway."

Reid joined the conversation. "If Hillman is working for what's left of the McFadden outfit, they could be trying to flush you out, boss. That goes for the tournament too."

Sparrow's nostrils flared as he exhaled. "How was she killed?"

I gave everyone a brief synopsis of the call. "Beckman said she didn't show up at the club. She doesn't live far. He thought she overslept and he went to her house."

"How did he get in?" Mason asked.

My head shook. I should have asked. "He didn't say. We'll find out at the club. He kept mentioning blood. Marcelo's team will tell us more. I got Beckman calmed enough, I hope. He said he'd stay and wait for the team and then meet me at the club."

Sparrow's head was shaking. "I don't like any of this." He looked at Mason and me. "Stop on two. I want you both prepared for anything."

We nodded.

"I'll stay here now," Sparrow said, though it was obvious it wasn't what he wanted. "I'm not sure about later. Right now, you two go and keep me and Reid updated. I'm putting the apartments on lockdown.

"Reid and I are in flux," Sparrow went on. "No matter what the risk, we'll be where we're needed. We need to assume her death was another arrow shot at us. My gut is telling me that Veronica's death is not only connected to the tournament but that it is more than likely connected to Hillman. Reid," Sparrow looked at him. "We know Hillman and his men went back to the hotel after their little house party. Are we sure they stayed?"

"I'll head down to two and see what I can find," Reid replied.

"Lockdown?" I asked in confirmation.

"Yes," Sparrow said. "Our job is out there. We'll all take precautions, but this is our city." He tilted his head toward the kitchen. "With them, I'm not taking any chances."

We all nodded.

"Okay, let's go," I said. As I spoke, Araneae came into the room.

"Sorry to interrupt. I just called Garrett," she said, giving Sparrow a kiss. "I know it's Saturday, but Laurel and I are headed to the foundation for a bit. She wants to check something and I have some paperwork..."

Mason, Reid, and I exchanged looks as the speed of our walking toward the elevator increased.

"Laurel and Lorna?" I asked when we arrived to the pocket door that disguised the elevator.

"I'm calling Lorna now," Reid said.

Mason had his phone out. "Yes, sending a text. I wasn't sticking around for Sparrow's announcement."

The three of us scoffed as we stepped into the elevator. I hit the button for two.

This was in no way a laughing matter. However, it was no secret how Sparrow's wife felt about lockdowns, even on a frigid Saturday morning. It wasn't that she'd make a scene in front of us, but we all knew that when Araneae had her chance, she'd relay her opinion to her husband in no uncertain terms. No matter the risk out in the world, Sparrow would get an earful, most likely delivered loud and clear.

MADELINE

With my phone in hand, I paced the length of my hotel room from the door to the window and back. I'd done it so many times, the carpeting was pockmarked from the indentation of my high heels. My breakfast tray was still lying upon the desk and the decanter of coffee was empty. The time on the screen of my phone read 10:20 a.m. The next round of the tournament would begin in less than two hours with or without me.

Pressing the speaker button, I tried Mitchell's cell phone for probably the twenty-fifth time. On my end, I heard three rings before it went to voicemail. Three. Each time it was the same, never varying. I disconnected, not leaving another message.

"Where are you?" I asked aloud, though no one could hear.

One more try.

I didn't bother to put it on speaker.

Besides the hum of the heat, the room was silent.

Three rings. 'Leave a message.'

I disconnected.

Gah.

Even Mitchell's voicemail was annoying. Couldn't he say *hello* or *you have reached...?*

I busied myself as much as I could in a hotel room to keep my mind off the impending tournament and Mitchell's absence. Entering the bathroom, I did another check of my hair and makeup.

Since I hadn't received specific dressing instructions from Andros, I'd done—as I did most days—managing my appearance on my own. My hair was down, curled in waves cascading down my back. The dress I wore was long and emerald green with a low-cut neckline and a slit along the side.

The plan all along had been for me to wear this particular one on the final day. Yes, I was a woman in a man's arena, but I wasn't above a bit of distraction. If my opponents were more interested in my cleavage than my cards, they only had themselves to blame.

I dabbed a bit of perfume between the swell of my breasts. As I did, my mind went to one of my possible opponents. Patrick's words came back to me, twisting my stomach and delivering a rush of warmth to my core.

'...know I'm thinking about how it feels to be inside you and the way you moan as I'm going down on you.'

I pouted my lips and ran another layer of gloss over the red stain. After I finished, I whispered, "I'm sorry, Patrick. I have to win."

I brought the screen of my phone back to life.

Shit!

It was now nearly ten thirty.

I stopped my pacing at the window. Peering out the large pane, I assessed traffic below. Late at night we had made it back to the Palmer House in less than fifteen minutes. This wasn't late at night. Despite the snow and cold, the city, stories below, was alive with people coming and going from here to there. Those wrapped from head to toe were along the sidewalk while vehicles of all sizes and colors filled the streets.

This was getting ridiculously close to bad form. I shouldn't show up at Club Regal just as play was about to begin.

I pushed dial and called Mitchell's phone again.

Three rings.

"Leave—"

Hitting disconnect, I threw my phone onto the bed.

This can't be happening. I hadn't gotten this far to not play out.

And then it hit me like a ton of bricks.

Oh my God. How had I been so stupid?

"Damn you, Patrick," I said to no one. "I will not forfeit. I will not cash out. That's not happening."

Was I paranoid or could Patrick somehow be responsible for Mitchell's delay?

Like everything else since returning to Chicago, I wasn't certain of anything.

That wasn't entirely true. I knew two things: I needed to get to Club Regal, and I needed to get there soon.

I pulled up my call log. If I had Patrick's number, I would call him and give him a piece of my mind. However, no matter the reason, Mitchell was the person missing in action. I didn't want to care, but in a small way I did. It wasn't like him and I was worried.

As my frustration grew, I had a twinge of sympathy for Andros the other night when I hadn't answered my phone.

Back to my call log.

I stopped on Andros's phone number. Truly it wasn't a number. It appeared blocked, yet I knew that from my phone, it was the call that would reach him.

If I were in Detroit, calling Andros was only permitted in the case of an emergency. The rules may not apply here, out of town, and then again, they may. There was no assuming when it came to Andros Ivanov. As each minute ticked away, I was convinced the situation was getting very close to emergency status.

Just as I was about to make the call, my phone rang, vibrating in my hand and setting my already-frayed nerves on edge.

Was it Mitchell or Andros?

Taking a deep breath, I read the screen.

UNKOWN NUMBER
DALLAS, TX

Was this Marion? Who else could it be?

How did he have my number?

I knew I hadn't given it to him. Then again, Andros had instructed me to distract him. I hoped that included on the phone. The second ring echoed off the walls.

"Hello," I said, doing my best to sound calm.

"Madeline, where are you?"

I let out an exaggerated breath. It was Marion. "I'm still in my hotel room. My driver hasn't arrived."

"No, that won't do at all. Most of the participants are already here. Although I have to say there is something happening. I was hoping to avoid the others and spend our time together."

"It seems that I'm stuck. I can't reach him."

"Where did you say you're staying? The Palmer House?"

Had I told him?

I could have. "Yes, the Palmer House."

"My driver will be there in twenty minutes. I'll tell him to break every law, but of course, not to be caught."

"I really shouldn't," I said. "I'm sure Mitchell is simply caught in traffic."

"If he arrives before Justin, call me and all is well. I have waited for years to challenge you in the final round of a tournament. Your name on the roster was what lured me to this tournament. I will not allow a late driver to interfere with my plans."

He'd entered because of me?

That was something that required more thought. Now wasn't the time. I was desperate, more desperate than I wanted to sound. "Marion, really, I will have the doorman call for a taxi cab."

"Nonsense. Justin is already on his way," Marion answered. "A woman as beautiful as you shouldn't arrive in a dirty cab but in style. Watch for the black Mercedes limousine. I apologize that it's rather small. The one I keep at home doesn't fit in my plane. You know how it is?"

My head shook. I didn't know how it was. Andros had money and liked his expensive toys, yet recently, I'd rarely been along for the ride. In most cases that suited me fine. "Thank you, Marion. I am very grateful."

"You will share dinner with me then, between the rounds."

"I don't—"

"It will be your way of saying thank you," he said.

The hairs on the back of my neck bristled. I already felt that I'd led him on too much. "I suppose that will depend if we both advance."

"I have no doubt. Watch for Justin. I'll see you soon."

"Marion?" I asked.

"Yes."

"How did you get my number?"

"I can't tell you all my secrets," he said with a smirk in his tone.

"Thank you again," I said as I disconnected the call.

Donning my winter coat, I swooped my long hair outside the collar and reached for my handbag. One last look in the mirror. "Whatever you did, Mr. Kelly, didn't work. I will arrive in time."

By the time I rode down in the elevator and walked through the lobby to the front door, my wait time was only a few minutes. One more time, I tried Mitchell's number. Three rings.

"Ms. Miller," the doorman said, bringing my attention to him.

"Yes."

"Ma'am, your ride is waiting."

Waiting? It hadn't been twenty minutes.

"Thank you," I sighed, grateful I would soon be in transit.

The car the doorman led me to had dark windows. It was also much larger than I expected, making me wonder how it fit into Marion's plane.

What kind of plane did he have?

"Ms. Miller?" a man in a chauffeur's uniform asked.

"Yes, and you're Justin?"

He smiled sweetly. "I am, ma'am." He reached for the door handle and opened the back door. "Mr. Elliott wanted me to assure him that you'll arrive on time. I think we should be fine."

"Yes," I said. "You arrived sooner than I expected."

"He told me to hurry."

I smiled as I took his hand. "Thank you." I stooped, stepping into the limousine. My shoes were both inside and the door closed. As I turned to sit, the man in the far seat with the dark hair and eyes came into view. My quick inhale stifled my gasp.

"My dear, we need to talk," his timbre was silky, but I knew it was just smooth enough to cover the thorns.

"Andros," I replied.

PATRICK

$\mathscr{T}$he tournament was set to begin in less than an hour and even with everything happening, I'd been watching for Madeline's arrival. Last time I was out in the club, she wasn't there. I didn't know why we hadn't exchanged phone numbers, but now I wish we had. Besides myself, the other sixteen players were present and accounted for. On the surface of Club Regal, all appeared normal.

Under the surface and behind the scenes, Ethan Beckman was ready to fall apart. He'd managed to pull himself together enough to make it out of his office and touch base with his employees, telling them that he hadn't been able to contact Veronica and he needed them all to fill in where needed.

Now he was with me, back in his office. "Our team," I told him, "agreed with what you said. There was a lot of blood. The splatter and pooling indicate that she was killed with one shot to the back of her head at close range. Due to the coagulation of the blood, body temperature, and stage of rigor mortis, they're estimating that she was killed six to ten hours earlier. I realize that's a wide range. Without tampering with the body more than they already did, it isn't an exact science. The coroner will be able to do more.

"Roughly with the estimate they provided, we can assume the time of death to be between ten o'clock last night and two o'clock this morning. What time did she leave here last night?"

I couldn't believe I hadn't tracked her down as I'd planned. If I had, I'd know the answer to this question.

Beckman's head shook. "I'm not sure. The tournament didn't end until eleven. She was here then."

"After that?" I asked.

"I'm sorry," he said, exasperated. "I should know, but this tournament has racked my nerves. I left as soon as I could." He looked up. "It was after the players who were eliminated were given the payout for their remaining chips. Do your people know anything else?"

"They found a 9mm cartridge," I said, "which means shit. It's one of the most popular handgun cartridges in the world. The team left it for the police. They might be able to get more information from it."

Beckman placed his elbows on his desk and laid his head in his hands. "Veronica has worked for me and for Club Regal for nearly twenty years." His chin rose until his bloodshot eyes met mine. "We've had our disagreements over that time, but dead? Who would do this?"

My head shook. "Do you know who carries in the club?"

"No. We have a don't ask, don't tell policy. It's unwritten. Illinois law requires a concealed carry license. It's been our policy that if the state allows it, who are we to stop it?"

"And you believe that everyone who carries has the license?"

He stood. "I'm not stupid, Mr. Kelly. I know that isn't true; however, it's the club policy." His eyes opened wide. "Do you think whoever did this to Veronica could be here now? Are we in danger?"

"We have Sparrows protecting the club and especially the tournament. The amount of money in that tournament is excessive."

"It's not in there." He tilted his head toward a safe on the floor behind his desk. "It's in here. All that's in the tournament hall are chips in place of money. They're worthless outside of this club."

"I want one of my men to stay in your office until the tournament is done and the money is distributed."

"That's highly unusual," he said.

"These are unusual circumstances. After all, it's not every day that one of your respected employees is murdered." I sat down on a chair opposite his desk. Leaning back, I crossed one ankle over a knee. "You said you argued recently. Tell me what you argued about."

"It's not important now."

"At this point, everything is important. Let me decide."

Beckman took a deep breath. "Veronica wasn't happy about the late buy-ins in this tournament."

I remembered our last conversation wherein Ms. Standish had expressed her disapproval of the buy-ins. I'd swiftly put an end to her complaints, saying I'd be happy to tell Sparrow she was questioning his decisions. Her face had turned ashen and she'd answered quickly..."*I respect Mr. Sparrow's decisions as does Mr. Beckman. Your entry isn't the one I'm concerned about.*"

"What was her concern?" I asked.

"She was afraid that allowing Mr. Hillman to buy in would create a precedent."

"Leading to more, like me?" I added.

"Yes, but Mr. Kelly, I'm not saying that she didn't want you in the tournament. That isn't...Mr. Sparrow...of course we were both willing to accommodate."

"Tell me why you were willing to accommodate Antonio Hillman."

Beckman sat taller. "He had been a member of this club in good standing for many years, as had his father..."

"Isn't the operative word *had*?"

"He asked," Beckman finally said.

The truth was that I hadn't asked. I'd simply informed him that since he'd allowed one buy-in, Mr. Sparrow had an offer. I supposed he could have refused, but very few refused a Sparrow offer. "I believe you're not telling me the entire story."

"Mr. Kelly, I don't want any trouble."

"Did Ms. Standish relay her displeasure to anyone else?" I asked.

"Not to my knowledge."

Could Hillman have discovered she wasn't supportive of his buy-in and taken it personally?

"Mr. Kelly, I just want this tournament to end and Veronica to walk through the door like she does almost every day."

"Tell me about Mr. Hillman's request."

"It was nothing." Beckman stood and paced a small trek behind his desk. "I-I..." He turned to me. "It was a long time ago."

"What was a long time ago?"

"It was before Mr. Sparrow...you know, before Senator McFadden was arrested."

"Go on," I prompted.

"Antonio's father helped me out of a tight spot. Hell, I'd almost forgotten about it."

"That doesn't seem like something you'd forget."

"When Mr. Antonio Hillman called, he reminded me. Allowing him to enter this tournament was a favor repaying his father's favor. You know, quid pro quo?"

"Why this particular tournament? Club Regal hosts many poker tournaments."

Beckman shook his head as he once again fell into his chair. "Mr. Kelly, I don't know. As I said, he asked for me to repay his father's favor."

"This is what is going to happen," I began. "First, you will allow the increased Sparrow security today and tonight."

He nodded.

"Second, you will allow one man to stay in here near the safe."

The pallor of his complexion grew even paler. "It's a safe. It can protect itself. Besides, only Veronica and I...only I know the combination."

Planting my feet firmly upon the floor, I leaned forward and asked, "Ms. Standish and you? No one else?"

"No, one of us was always here."

I looked over toward the safe. "Have you opened it today?"

"Well...no... I...with all that's happened..."

We both looked again toward the safe. Black and about four feet tall, it appeared heavy, and from a previous meeting, I knew it was bolted to the concrete floor. With the door closed, it appeared untouched.

"Do it," I said. "Open it. I hate to think that Ms. Standish lost her life over money, but if the murderer's goal was accessing what's in the safe, we need to verify that the money is present."

Visibly shaken, Beckman stood, turned, and crouched down beside the safe, blocking the keypad from my view.

Five beeps preceded the sound of the door opening. I stood.

"Oh my God…" he wailed. "It's gone."

We now had motive.

"How much was in there?"

When he turned his eyes were glassy. "With buy-ins, entry fees, and the purchased chips…" Standing quickly, he pushed past me. "I'm going to be sick."

The retching from the attached bathroom confirmed his prediction.

I began my text to Sparrow, Reid, and Mason. While Mason was out in the club, he wouldn't know what I'd just learned.

"MS. STANDISH KNEW THE COMBINATION OF THE CLUB'S SAFE. BECKMAN JUST CONFIRMED THE CASH FROM THE TOURNAMENT IS GONE."

I hit send as Beckman returned with a bit more color in his cheeks than he'd had before. "How much?" I asked again.

"Veronica had the paperwork. The players who were eliminated have been reimbursed for their chips. What was here was from the remaining players."

My volume rose. "How much?"

"I don't know for sure. I would guess upward of fifteen million."

"Who knew that she knew the combination?"

"Probably most of the employees," he said.

My phone buzzed. The text was from Sparrow.

"HOW MUCH?"

I replied with the amount I'd been told. And then I looked up. "Mr. Beckman, you can't tell anyone that it's missing. No one."

"But...but how? Club Regal will be ruined." He resumed his pacing. "This will get out that we weren't able to repay...worldwide, we'll be ostracized. No one will come here after this. Our reputation will be destroyed."

I was hearing what Beckman was saying, but my impression was different. This wouldn't only reflect negatively on Club Regal. It would reflect poorly on the Sparrow outfit. We were here to maintain the safety. This money was stolen right from under our noses. That information would be another dagger for McFadden's men or any other outfit to use against us. If we couldn't protect this tournament, it will be assumed that we also can't protect our city.

"Mr. Beckman, look at me," I demanded.

Slowly he did.

"Does the safe maintain a record of when it is opened and who opened it?"

"No...it...was just the two of us...We only had one

combination." His head shook. "Oh my God." His eyes met mine. "Why her and not me?"

"That's a good question," I said. "Close the safe and lock it. I will still put a man back here to keep guard. We will provide the illusion of normalcy to everyone behind the scenes. Do not repeat this information. Do not say a word about the money or the safe or that Ms. Standish knew the combination. Do not speak of this to *anybody*." I emphasized the word. "Do you understand?"

"No? I don't understand. What will happen at the end of the tournament?"

My phone vibrated. The text was from Sparrow.

"THIS CAN'T GET OUT. WE'LL COVER THE LOSS."

I looked up. "Find out the exact amount that was taken. Give that information to Mr. Pierce. Mr. Sparrow will assure that this isn't the disaster that it could be. Do not tell a soul, Mr. Beckman. If it is leaked, you will regret it."

I sent another text to the team.

"CHECK ALL COMINGS AND GOINGS FROM CLUB REGAL LAST NIGHT UNTIL THIS MORNING. WE NEED TO KNOW WHEN MS. STANDISH LEFT THE CLUB AND IF SHE RETURNED. ALSO, CAN YOU ACCESS VIEWS FROM HER BUILDING OR THE STREET? WHO CAME AND

WENT FROM HER BUILDING OR HER APARTMENT? WE NEED ANSWERS."

Before I could get a response, I sent one more.

"WE ALSO NEED TO KNOW WHERE BECKMAN WAS LAST NIGHT. HE SAID HE LEFT AFTER THE TOURNAMENT PAYOUTS. PHONE RECORDS. TRAFFIC CAMS. ANYTHING YOU CAN FIND."

Beckman still hadn't told me what favor Wendell Hillman did for him years ago. His question about why her and not him could have been meant to throw us off or he may have unwittingly sent me in the right direction. Regardless, I didn't trust that he wasn't more involved.

Another text came through to me. This one was from Sparrow, but no longer part of the group text.

"GO ALL IN ON THE FINAL GAME. WIN IT ALL."

MADELINE

*T*he smile was plastered upon my lips as Marion met his car near the curb, ready to escort me inside Club Regal. Andros said not to mention his presence to Marion. I couldn't comprehend what was happening.

Why had Andros Ivanov been in Marion's limousine?

"You made it," he gushed as he helped me from the back seat. "Nice work, Justin," he said with a tip of his head to the driver.

"Thank you, Mr. Elliott."

I didn't notice the cold air on the sidewalk or even the warmth as we entered the club's entrance. There was too much to comprehend.

"Madeline?"

I looked up at Marion's wrinkled face, the way small lines formed at the sides of his eyes as he smiled. My head tilted. His eyes were blue. I hadn't noticed them before. They weren't the same as Patrick's blue. Marion's were pale in comparison.

"Little lady, are you all right?" he asked.

"I'm sorry. I believe I'm flustered."

"Of course you are. Your driver should be fired. This treatment of a beautiful woman is unacceptable and especially before the tournament. Tell me the service you hired, and I will have the man fired myself."

My head shook. "Marion, I'd rather not think about it." I'd rather not think that Andros ordered Mitchell to leave Chicago, unconcerned that in the process he'd left me stranded. When I asked him why he sent Mitchell away, Andros said it wasn't my concern.

Nothing is my concern except winning, winning it all.

When I asked why I hadn't been informed and had been left stranded, he dismissed me as if I were a bothersome child seeking his attention.

The truth was that I didn't want his attention. I wanted to go back to Detroit and fade into the woodwork where I'd been. Though Andros hadn't used the exact words, I had come to the realization years ago that I was nothing more than a plaything to Andros, a doll to be removed from the shelf, dusted off, and given a new layer of paint before showing me off to his friends and enemies. "Look what my doll can do. Watch her win the hands of poker. Watch as she does as I command."

"Madeline, let me help you with your coat," Marion said. "We have a little time before the tournament. Perhaps a glass of wine will help calm your nerves?"

I unfastened the large buttons on the front of my winter coat. As Marion reached to help me remove it, he let out a low hiss.

"That dress," he said.

The smile returned. I had a job to do, and I needed to do as Andros had said and stay focused. "This?" I asked coyly. "I hope you like it."

"You're stunning. How will I ever be able to concentrate on the cards?"

"Maybe that's my plan."

Marion laughed. "The rumors are correct."

"Rumors?" I asked.

"As I said before, beautiful, mysterious, and lethal."

I placed my hand on his sleeve as he led me into Bar Regal.

When the waitress approached, Marion ordered our drinks. "A glass of chardonnay for the lady and Glen Marnoch neat for me."

"Really," I protested. "Water is all."

Marion winked her way. "Bring the lady both."

"Yes, sir. Right away."

"Marion, I must protest. Getting me tipsy before the tournament would affect my concentration."

"Perhaps, that is my plan. If you can make me and all the other players drunk with lust in that green dress that matches your emerald eyes, I can return the favor."

After the waitress delivered our drinks, Marion raised his glass. "A toast."

I lifted the glass of wine in kind. "To what should we toast?"

"To each of our successes." Our glasses clinked.

"And don't forget," he said after a sip of his whiskey, "we have a table reserved for dinner."

"I'd like to reserve a seat near you at the poker table in tonight's finals," I said with a grin.

"I'm not sure it's done that way, but I believe we will both find ourselves there."

I leaned closer. "I have a secret."

"Oh? Little lady, do tell."

"I'm going to win it all."

The sharing of my secret earned me a hearty laugh.

As I was about to take another drink, a man I recognized from the tournament approached our table. "Ms. Miller, Mr. Elliott, I wanted to introduce myself. I'm Ethan Beckman. I will be overseeing today's rounds of the tournament."

"Where is Ms. Standish?" Marion asked.

Mr. Beckman's expression changed for only a microsecond. "I haven't seen her yet today and well, play must go on." He turned to me. "Speaking of which, Ms. Miller, I'm relieved that you arrived."

"Yes. I'm sorry," I said. "I don't usually like to cut it so close."

He smiled. "It is all well now that you're here." He turned to Mr. Elliott and back to me. "If you two will join us, it's time to begin today's first round." He looked at our drinks. "Leave them. We have plenty upstairs."

Once Mr. Beckman had walked away, Marion whispered. "I'm at the disadvantage."

"And why is that?"

"You're still wearing that magnificent dress, and you only took one sip of your wine. We can rectify that at dinner."

With my hand again on his arm, we made our way up the grand stairs. As we neared the top, a different set of blue eyes met mine. Unlike Marion's, this set sent a spark to my skin, warming me inside and out. It would be so easy to remember what it was like to see those eyes every day.

"Mr. Kelly," Marion said. "Good luck in there today."

Patrick offered his hand and the two shook.

"Have you met our gorgeous competitor, Ms. Miller?"

Patrick's gaze met mine as he again offered his hand.

My breathing stilled. That was the same hand that had roamed my skin last night, the same fingers that had brought me pleasure and held tightly to my hips. I reached out.

"Ms. Miller."

"Mr. Kelly."

I doubted that Marion noticed how my hand lingered in Patrick's or observed the unspoken conversation, but by the way my heart raced and hand tingled from our connection, I was aware of everything about the encounter and more. I looked Patrick up and down, from the gleam in his eyes to the way his suit fit over his broad shoulders and wide chest. I recalled what it was like to lie in his embrace, to run my fingers over the indentations of his abdomen.

I told myself it was simply the return of a childhood crush and that being in his presence had brought it back with a vengeance. It was the lie I repeated, knowing it could never be more. It wasn't possible.

Warmth crawled up my neck, no doubt bringing pink to my skin as I remembered what he said he'd be thinking when he saw me. Yes, Patrick, I was thinking the same thing, too.

I retrieved my hand.

"Lady and gentlemen," Mr. Beckman called over our murmurs. "Please come inside. We're ready to begin seat selection."

"Good luck, gentlemen," I said as I stepped away, entering the hall alone.

I needed the break.

It was time to concentrate.

Eighteen of us stood as names were drawn, one by one filling the chairs at the three remaining tables. A gallery of additional chairs had been set up where other tables had once been. No longer did our observers need to stand. The tournament was more than a game for those of us playing. We were now on display, the entertainment for members of the club.

"Ms. Madeline Miller," the announcer said.

Smiling, I made my way toward the middle table. Marion had already been seated at the first table, along with Mr. Garcia and four other players.

"Mr. Antonio Hillman."

I nodded to the man taking the seat to my left. As I did, I noticed Patrick, still standing. It seemed as though something about this placement had Patrick's attention.

"It's nice to meet you, Ms. Miller," Mr. Hillman said with a smile.

My head tilted. "Have we met?" He seemed vaguely familiar.

"Only crossed paths."

I hummed.

"Last night you were seated at a table near me," he clarified.

"Yes," I said. "I'm sure that's it. Good luck, Mr. Hillman."

"Please, Antonio."

"Then call me Madeline."

When I looked around, all players were seated. Patrick was at the last table with his five other opponents. Truly, at this stage all the players were our opponents. We had until four o'clock to win enough to earn a seat at the final table.

"Shall we begin?" our dealer asked.

PATRICK

J was in fucking hell, trapped like a performer on a stage, unable to do what I did—investigate and help. And by the way Mason was texting on his phone, I knew more was happening, more than Veronica Standish and the missing fifteen million. And that was a lot. On top of that, Hillman had been seated beside Madeline. I couldn't see how their hands of poker were going or updates on my phone. All I could see were the cards.

"GO ALL IN. WIN IT ALL."

No pressure.

"Mr. Kelly," our dealer said, "the bet's to you. The call is fifteen."

I was tired of the meager bets. Three of my opponents

placed in lower earnings than I had in the last round. The other two had placed higher. Because placement was based on winnings per round, not accumulated earnings, I hadn't known exactly what I'd be up against. I did know that I placed tenth and I needed to move up to the top six.

My cards were shit—A, J, J, 6, 4. We still had the draw and it was time to take matters into my own hands. "I see your $15,000, and raise another twenty-five."

Murmurs came from my opponents as well as some of the people watching.

What did they know?

They couldn't see my cards.

"That is forty to you..." the dealer said as he went around the table.

With one fold, play continued with five players.

My opponents had taken anything from one card to the maximum of three.

"Mr. Kelly?"

Handing over the 6 and 4, facedown, I collected two more cards. I wasn't a big fan of holding a kicker, but it was difficult with a hand like the one I held to throw away an ace.

I peeled back the corner of the first card.

10.

Shit.

"Mr. Kelly, it's your bet."

I didn't speak as I peeled back the corner of the second card. Ace.

I looked up to the anticipation of my opponents. Counting out five stacks, I pushed them forward. "Fifty."

"The bet is $50,000," the dealer repeated.

My first opponent folded. The second took his time before throwing in his cards. It was the third, Mr. Julius Dunn, who continued play. From Reid and Mason's research, I'd learned Dunn was little more than a playboy, the jet-set type with the perpetual tan—even in Chicago in January—and the whiter-than-white smile.

"What the hell," Mr. Dunn said as he pushed $50,000 in chips forward. "And I raise you ten."

The last opponent folded.

I added ten more to the pot.

It was the responsibility of the last person who bet or raised to show his cards. That meant that with his $10,000 raise, Mr. Dunn had put himself in the spotlight, a place I'd decided he enjoyed.

"Mr. Dunn," the dealer said.

Mr. Dunn's million-dollar smile grew. "Two pair."

I nodded.

He turned over two jacks.

I didn't need to respond. I didn't even need to show my cards, not if I wasn't claiming victory. However, this was more. I needed to show the world I didn't bluff. I turned over my pair of jacks. "Go on," I said.

At the appearance of my pair of jacks, the wattage of Mr. Dunn's smile dimmed a bit.

"Your other pair, Mr. Dunn?" the dealer asked.

He turned over his three remaining cards—8, 8, A. "Just in case you planned on replicating my pair of eights, too," he said.

"I wasn't." I flipped over my pair of aces.

The crowd aahed.

With a nod, I raked in the pot. In one hand I'd accumulated over $200,000.

Yes, that was the way it was supposed to work.

As the dealer shuffled our deck, the crowd again aahed. I looked up in time to watch as Madeline pulled a large pile of chips her direction.

Cash out.

It was my first thought, and then I remembered Sparrow's text. Madeline cashing out would cost the Sparrow outfit. He'd want her to lose it all.

No matter what was happening, I didn't want that.

More hands came and went. I won and I lost. Glancing at my watch, I saw that we had less than a half hour of play remaining. My table was down to four players. We'd lost two through normal attrition. They'd bet all they could and lost.

That possibility was why this was called gambling.

While the victories moved around the table, the tall stacks belonged to me and Mr. Dunn.

Finally, the call came from the announcer. "Lady and gentlemen, this hand concludes this session's play."

I looked around, wondering where Beckman was, but I couldn't locate him.

The dealer lifted his hands. He'd been shuffling. That meant our table was done.

I waited impatiently while our chips were counted and the amounts were verified. Two players had left earlier with nothing. From the looks of the stacks, another two from my table would not make the next round. Each appeared to have less than $50,000. Those were payouts that wouldn't cause Sparrow to balk. Under normal circumstances, it would be a fraction of the taxes paid.

These weren't normal circumstances.

My gaze met Mason's. Wordlessly, I asked if cash had been restored to the safe. It would be needed as the non-advancing players cashed out.

He nodded.

"Mr. Kelly," the dealer said, handing me my receipt.

I read the total. It wasn't a shock. I'd been keeping track.

$2,600,000

Minus the players who had already stepped away from their table, the rest of us remained seated as the room grew deadly quiet. The man who had announced the end of play collected the totals.

I'd begun the round with $350,000. That meant I'd earned $2,250,000. It better be enough.

"We will begin with our sixth addition to the final round."

The room took a collective breath.

"Mr. Nicholas Garcia."

The room filled with applause.

"Mr. Julius Dunn."

More applause.

"Ms. Madeline Miller."

My eyes closed as the crowd applauded. Damn, this would be easier if she could just cash out.

"Mr. Antonio Hillman."

My gaze went to Mason's. His stare was set on Hillman, and if I were to guess, he wasn't happy.

"Mr. Patrick Kelly."

I nodded as I too received applause.

The final name was expected, but then again, nothing was certain.

"Mr. Marion Elliott."

The applause gave way to voices, everyone talking.

"Ladies and gentlemen," the announcer said, now speaking to the entirety of the room, "we will resume play at seven o'clock sharp. Once the doors close they will not reopen until the play is complete."

Taking my receipt, I placed it in my inside jacket pocket as I stood. While I searched for Madeline, Mason appeared at my side.

"Come with me. It's a shit show."

MADELINE

a tall and intimidating-looking man with a short ponytail near his neck hurried to Patrick's side after the finalists had been announced. There was something about the man that made me nervous, worrying that Patrick was somehow in danger.

"Congratulations," Antonio said as he started to stand. "May I buy you a drink?"

"The lady's with me."

I didn't need to turn. I recognized the drawl.

I forced a smile. "It's not a big club. I'm sure we'll see one another," I said to Antonio. "Marion and I do have plans for dinner."

Antonio nodded. Standing, he offered Marion his hand. "It's nice to have your backing."

"I like to help when I can," Marion said as they shook.

My gaze went from one to the other. I had the feeling I was back in Detroit as Andros conducted a secret meeting in my presence. Deals were made. Favors granted. Hands greased. Assets were acquired, yet it all happened on an alternative plane, just outside the obvious.

When Antonio walked away, I asked, "So you know him?"

"We've met." His eyes shone. "Let's go downstairs and have dinner. Winning always makes me hungry."

"Where have you met?"

We were now walking toward the stairs. As we did, I searched about looking for Patrick, but he was out of sight, not out of mind.

"It's very boring," Marion said. "Tell me about your wins. From eighth place to fourth is impressive."

"Thank you. Don't sell yourself short. Maintaining first is no easy feat." I peered down the hall toward the bathrooms where I'd first seen Patrick. It was only a few days before, but it seemed much longer.

In reality it was—a lifetime.

A few days ago wasn't the first time I saw him. That was nearly twenty years ago. I stilled. "Marion, if you'll excuse me for a moment. I will be happy to meet you downstairs."

"I'll wait right here," he said. "They will hold our table."

With a nod, I turned toward the hallway. Being a Saturday, there were more rooms in use than there had been on Thursday. I slowed at the sound of voices. The door was closed, yet there was a heated discussion happening within. No, it wasn't a discussion. It sounded as if someone was being questioned. Curiosity slowed my steps, yet I didn't recognize the voices.

They were saying something about a woman. I heard the name Veronica.

Veronica Standish?

She hadn't been in the tournament.

What was happening?

During our ride, Andros assured me that as long as I did my job, a car would pick me up after the tournament. My room was being packed and we were headed back to Detroit. While I would like to see Patrick one more time, it wouldn't be.

Once inside the restroom, I removed my phone and sent Andros a text message.

"I THOUGHT YOU'D WANT TO KNOW. I ADVANCED TO FOURTH PLACE."

I hit send.

It didn't take long until my phone vibrated. It was Andros.

"I WAS INFORMED. YOUR JOB ISN'T COMPLETE."

How did he know without Mitchell reporting?

Who was watching?

I read his text again. I knew my job wasn't complete even without his constant reminders. The thing about Andros that I'd come to learn was that he was a fan of quid pro quo. When I won the tournament, he would allow me what I desire most. I didn't and he'd deny me.

The thought tugged at my chest as I replied.

• • •

"I KNOW. I WON'T DISAPPOINT YOU."

My finger hovered over the send button. I wished I knew it was true. What was true was that I would do my best not to disappoint. Andros wouldn't want to hear that. He liked finality.

I hit send.

As I made my way back to the stairs, the door where I'd heard voices opened and the man who I'd seen with Patrick walked out. He was even taller closer up. His face was handsome, but there was something else about him that made me shiver. Without even a nod my direction, he walked farther down the hallway, away from the poker hall and stairs.

Was Patrick inside?

I hadn't recognized his voice, but I couldn't resist checking.

I waited until the tall man turned a corner and went to the door. Leaning my ear closer, I listened. There was no noise inside. My pulse kicked up a notch as I reached for the handle. It wouldn't budge. The door was locked. "Patrick?" I whispered into the doorjamb.

Silence.

The stress of this tournament, seeing Patrick, and Andros's arrival were officially making me paranoid. I looked down at my phone. I had one unread message.

It was from Andros.

"I'M COUNTING ON IT. FINISH YOUR JOB IF YOU PLAN TO RETURN."

. . .

If I planned to return?

The thought of not was too painful to entertain.

I knew the scenario too well. It was Andros's power and he wouldn't hesitate to wield it over me. I didn't need to reply. He knew my answer. I would win and accompany him back to Detroit.

Shaking my head, I placed my phone back into my purse.

Marion was waiting where he said he'd be at the top of the stairs. As I took his arm and we descended the stairs, in the crowd below, I saw the same man from the hallway.

"There must be other stairs," I said.

"Not that I've seen. Why?" Marion asked.

"See that tall man in the light-gray suit?" I tipped my head to the main floor. "He was up here and left in a hurry the other direction."

"Interesting," Marion said.

The hostess sat us at a table near the large fireplace. The chairs were large Queen Anne-style and covered in red leather. Similar to other parts of the Club Regal, the walls were covered in rich cherry paneling and large tapestries and pieces of artwork hung on long wires secured to the ceiling above. Even the ceiling was ornate, white with cherry accent.

"This is lovely," I said, noticing Antonio Hillman seated with three other men at a table across the room. "How did you say you met Mr. Hillman?"

"A long time ago. He wasn't more than a teenager. It was his father I knew. His father helped me with a few issues I was having with my companies. I'm always happy to repay a favor."

There was something in his tone that set my nerves on edge. I'd been right about the brief conversation I overheard. What

Marion was saying was Andros's quid pro quo from the other side. I decided to change the subject. "Thank you again for sending the car. Your driver was nice."

Marion set down his water glass and looked around. "That is good to hear. You see, Justin isn't my regular driver. Unfortunately, just before this trip, my driver became ill and unable to accompany me. As you can imagine, it was a disaster."

I wasn't certain it qualified as a disaster. There were actual disasters I could list.

When I didn't respond, Marion went on. "I called Mr. Beckman, the man who spoke to us earlier..."

I nodded.

"He offered to set me up with a reliable driver. Much more reliable than yours, I'd say."

"Yes."

Did Marion know that Andros was in his car?

Or was his presence coordinated by the driver assigned by Mr. Beckman?

"I'm so thankful you sent him." I looked up at his eyes. "Who was it that you said gave you my phone number? I'm grateful to them and to you."

"Then I won't share," Marion said. "I'd prefer to keep your gratitude to myself."

PATRICK

*T*he world had gone mad. While I had been upstairs playing poker, there'd been an explosion at the docks. A shipping container that had been delivered a day earlier exploded. The container was supposed to be filled with building supplies for a chain store. The police were on the scene and two people were injured.

The police had also responded to the anonymous call and discovered Veronica's body. During the tournament, a detective had made a preliminary visit to Club Regal and spoke to Ethan Beckman. According to the capo stationed in Beckman's office, the meeting had been short and Beckman had shown the appropriate amount of shock. The detective left his card and promised to return to speak to the other employees on a less busy day.

Reid had followed up on Mitchell Leonardo. There was no sign of him returning to the Palmer House and he hadn't shown up today at Club Regal. The last time he'd been seen was when he was being picked up for the house party. That was before Reid was able to isolate another car that had been at the house party and was able to track it to a location near Veronica's residence.

The timing fit our forensics' information. The car stopped and the man who Reid believed to be Leonardo got out a few blocks from her house at 1:52 in the morning.

During the night and early morning, the falling snow had picked up. That wasn't helping the graininess of the images from the traffic cameras or satellite. It also didn't help with recognition. Winter coats and hats don't differ that much. From what Reid could tell, the car continued driving around the neighborhood until about fifteen minutes later; it stopped and picked up a man who could be Leonardo a quarter mile away.

We were making some assumptions based on the lack of foot traffic at two in the morning.

There was no sign of that car coming near the club. Therefore, if Leonardo did in fact kill Veronica, he didn't return to empty the safe. That didn't mean he couldn't have called or texted the combination to an accomplice.

One issue was that Club Regal remained open on Friday night until three o'clock Saturday morning. While no one entered the club after closing, there were more than he could track during operating hours. Some employees didn't leave until nearly four a.m.

Mason and another capo had been questioning a few of the employees who had been at the club later in the night as they arrived back to work today. While we'd usually do that kind of thing on level one in our tower, today we were making Club

Regal our temporary command center. So far, no one had information that stood out.

During the earlier round of play, Sparrow had arrived. He said he was fully protected, and his place was here, not held up in the tower. If shit was going to happen, it was his place as king of the city to be involved. He hadn't gotten his power by hiding behind others.

While I believed him, I suspected he was also avoiding a certain blonde who shared his last name, at least until the lockdown could be lifted.

Sparrow had commandeered Beckman's office while secluding Beckman to one of the other offices with a capo stationed outside the door. That explained why Beckman hadn't been the one to close out the early round. Sparrow said he wasn't comfortable with how frayed Beckman seemed when he arrived. 'Off-balanced' was the term he used. The last time I saw Beckman he'd blown chunks. Having Mr. Sparrow stare you down could make anyone off-balanced. Add seeing your employee with a hole in her head, and I supposed he deserved a little slack.

The only person still in the tower besides the women was Reid. It was the technology. He could do much more on two than if he were here.

"How much cash were you able to put your hands on?" I asked, looking at the safe.

"Twelve million," Sparrow said, "but the players who cashed out took over two hundred grand of it. If I had more time I could get the rest. I showed you the receipts from upstairs. This 11.8 won't cover it. You need to win it all."

My mind went to Madeline. If she cashed out now, she'd have

more than enough to live for a while. When Sparrow showed me the receipts, I looked at her total. She was sitting with around two million. If only I could talk to her.

The door opened. Mason walked in and sat in the chair beside me with a sigh. "The employees we've spoken to didn't see anything out of the ordinary. They all confirm they saw Ms. Standish after the tournament, but no one recalls after that."

"What about Beckman?" Sparrow asked.

"He told me why he allowed Hillman's entry," I said, it being my first chance to talk since tournament play began earlier today.

Sparrow leaned back in Beckman's chair. "Go on."

"He said Hillman's father did a favor for him years ago. When the younger Hillman called, he reminded Beckman of it."

Sparrow scoffed. "I'm sure he did."

Reid's image was on a laptop Sparrow had brought from our command center. It was like having him in the same room and the connection was secure. "I'm trying to access Leonardo's phone records to see if he called anyone after the time of Ms. Standish's death. The problem is that I'm not finding a phone registered to him."

"What about Ms. Miller?" Mason asked.

"What about her?" I replied.

"They've been together," Mason said. "Remember, they've arrived at and left the club together. We determined they were both staying at the Palmer House—"

"In separate rooms," I said.

Sparrow's dark gaze narrowed. "You learned that when you were checking out a lead there."

It wasn't a question, but I answered. "We talked about it

before. The thought was that Leonardo was her driver. I remember the word *goon* was used."

"Anyway," Mason went on, "wouldn't they have called one another? Can't you check her phone records to find Leonardo's?"

Reid nodded.

I fought the urge to pace or move. I didn't like the idea of them researching Madeline. If Leonardo was working for or with Hillman, my guess was that he somehow got himself assigned to Madeline as an in to the tournament. It was like when I was Araneae's driver. She didn't know anything about the Sparrow outfit. Madeline was in the same situation.

"Here's something interesting," Reid said through the computer screen.

We all turned and stared at the laptop. "What?" Sparrow asked.

"Patrick, you always say to follow the money. Remember me saying how Hillman's expenses were being funneled through a shell company?" He didn't wait for us to answer. "Leonardo's and Miller's are too."

The hairs on the back of my neck stood to attention. "The same one?"

"No but damn close. Addresses are PO boxes in Delaware. I couldn't find a phone registered to her either. I went to their hotel reservations. You were right, separate rooms. Anyway, nothing leads to either one of them."

"How about a work record on Leonardo?" I asked. "What driving company does he work for?"

"Not a driving company," Reid said. "He works for a construction company in Detroit."

"And he seconds as a driver who wasn't driving," Mason said.

"What?"

"Yeah, on the video of outside the club, Ms. Miller arrived with Leonardo at her side in a taxi. She left the same way."

"Except today," Reid volunteered. "The limousine had Texas plates and is registered to Elliott, Inc."

"Fuck," Sparrow said. "Elliott, Inc. We brushed on this the other day. I know that guy was kissing up to McFadden. I remember a big bill a few years ago. It was in the news outlets about the lobbyists and all the money going to..." He stopped and pulled out his phone. A moment later he nodded, staring down at the screen. "Yes, this is why I remember it. Marion Elliott wanted sanctions lifted on offshore drilling. In exchange, he worked out a deal to build a manufacturing plant in McKinley Park. It brought not only construction jobs but after it was built, it employed five hundred blue-collar workers and seventy-five or more in management with higher salaries. McFadden used it as a platform."

"What construction company got the bid?" I asked.

"Give me a minute," Reid said.

We all waited.

"Ivanov Construction," Reid said, "in Dearborn, Michigan."

"Where did you say Leonardo works?" Sparrow said.

"Other than driving," Reid answered, "Ivanov Construction."

My eyes met Sparrow's.

"Fucking Detroit," the two of us said together.

"Fill me in, man," Mason said.

Sometimes it was easy to forget Mason had been out of our loop for a while. It was probably because he fit back in so well that it was easy to forget he'd been gone. "Ivanov, Andros Ivanov," I said.

"He made some noise a few years ago," Sparrow said. "It was one of the few times McFadden and I worked together. Cut that shit out before it could grow."

"So if Hillman and his goons were at the house party with Leonardo..." I began.

"And Leonardo is connected to Ivanov..." Mason continued.

"Hillman wouldn't come in here all loud and obnoxious if he didn't have some power behind him," Sparrow said. "I know Elliott used to deal with McFadden. He hasn't made a bid my way."

"Maybe someone else got to him first," Reid said. "And someone got to Hillman. If we're right, Ivanov could be enticing McFadden's people, the ones we didn't get."

"Wait a minute," I said, "how does Madeline fit into this equation?"

"Madeline?" Sparrow said, his dark gaze again narrowing.

My head shook. "Ms. Miller."

"Maybe she found out Leonardo is dirty. He could have petitioned a job with her to be here," Mason offered.

It was what I'd been thinking.

"Or she's connected," he went on. "I mean, what do we really know about her?"

"How does this all connect to this tournament?" I asked.

"This tournament is a guise to get all the players here at once, check out the city, look for vulnerability," Sparrow said. "If I were thinking of taking over another city, that's what I'd do. Small jobs, chaos, and disruptions..."

"Like at the shipyard today," Reid said.

"And I'd get as close to the kingpin as possible," Sparrow

went on. "If that's the case, look what we've done. We're fucking playing into their hands."

"So the tournament doesn't matter," I said.

"Someone stole Club Regal's money—fifteen million. The tournament matters," Sparrow said.

"Andros Ivanov has been radio silent for the last twenty-four hours," Reid said. "He likes the shiny things—cars, planes, and women. Usually he's showboating on social media or the rags are posting his picture."

"If he's in my city, I want to know," Sterling said. He turned to me. "Win it all, as much as you can. I'm sure as hell not financing a coup against Sparrow."

"I need to come clean about something," I said, standing.

"Win the pot and jackpot and then tell me," Sparrow said. "I trust you with my life. Is this a reason I shouldn't?"

It wasn't. I'd pledged my loyalty to Sparrow and the outfit. That wasn't changing. I shook my head. "No."

"Let's send out Sparrows and find out if we're on to something. If we are, Detroit is in for a war. The casualties won't be in my city," Sparrow said.

MADELINE

$\mathcal{A}$s Marion and I walked up the stairs toward the poker hall, the excitement was palpable. Club Regal was nearly at capacity. The tournament had drawn poker lovers from around the city and beyond. The attendees stared and whispered as we passed by. It was a strange sensation to be so closely scrutinized by strangers. I was ready to win and go home. I was ready to go back to being invisible.

"Ms. Miller," a woman said, reaching for my arm.

"Yes?"

"I believe in you. I have $50,000 on you for the win."

My eyes opened wide. "I didn't realize the club was taking side bets."

"No, not the club. You're coming off at six to one in Vegas."

"Oh, I didn't realize."

Six to one. That meant for every dollar bet the win would be six. A $50,000 bet would gross $300,000.

Her smile grew. "Do it for the women. We're all counting on you."

"I will do my best."

"Madeline," Marion encouraged while giving me an escape.

With a nod to the other woman, he and I continued our ascent to the second floor.

"Did you know about that?" I asked Marion in a stage whisper.

"Yes, I have money riding on the tournament too."

"You bet on a tournament you're in?"

"I enjoy gambling. I especially enjoy it if I can win." He leaned closer. "I bet on myself. If I weren't a competitor, I would have put my money on you. My odds aren't nearly as lucrative."

Of course they weren't.

We were now at the top of the steps. The butterflies I sometimes felt flittering in my stomach before a final round were now the size of bats. "Marion, if you'll excuse me? I need a moment before the play begins."

He reached for my hand. "Thank you for eating dinner and spending time with me, Madeline. It has been a real pleasure to get to know the woman behind the myth."

My cheeks rose as a smile formed. "Hardly a myth. You're a legend."

"I would like to see you again, after the tournament," he said, still holding my hand.

"I don't know what the future will bring," I replied honestly. Whatever it entailed was as always at Andros's discretion. "I have responsibilities that won't allow me to stay here or make an unplanned trip to Dallas anytime soon."

"I wanted to ask," he said, "before we became competitors again. I believe I have the capital to win, and I wouldn't want that to influence your decision for the future."

My head tilted. "I'm glad you mentioned that. Otherwise I wouldn't know if you felt the same way after I won."

The lines formed around his eyes as he chuckled. "Time will tell. I'll see you across the table."

"Yes."

"And I can still hope for the future," he added.

With my handbag in hand, I made my way through the crowd toward the bathrooms. If I'd hoped for one more private encounter with Patrick, it wasn't to be. Even the ladies' room had occupants. As I was washing my hands, a new woman entered.

"Ms. Miller?"

"Yes," I said, drying my hands and hoping this wasn't another person telling me she'd placed money on me. As if the pressure from Andros wasn't enough.

The woman reached into her purse and handed me a folded piece of paper. "I was asked to deliver this to you."

I took it and read the script: **Ms. Miller.**

I opened the paper.

We don't have much time. Please see me. Go down the hallway, farther away from the poker room. The third door on the left. I must talk to you before we begin.

Patrick

. . .

I folded the paper and took one last look in the mirror. My gut told me not to do it, but my heart wouldn't let me miss this one last chance.

Moving away from the crowds, I followed Patrick's directions and counted the doors.

One.

Two.

Three.

The club was much quieter the farther I moved from the people. It was so quiet that I became oddly aware of the beating of my own heart as my circulation thumped in my ears. The bats in my stomach did flips and aerial acrobatics as I reached for the knob. The room inside was dim. It was the scent of his cologne that I recognized before his presence came into view. Large hands reached for my upper arms.

"You're fucking stunning tonight, Maddie."

I leaned toward him; his warmth filled me as we stood with my breasts against his solid chest. There were so many things I wanted to say. The most important was on the tip of my tongue, yet it wouldn't budge. It couldn't. That knowledge would change his world forever. I wasn't any more willing to accept that responsibility now than I had been before.

"I'm glad you sent the note," I said. "I'm leaving immediately after the tournament. I wanted to say goodbye."

His touch moved upward until his hands were at my cheeks gently lifting my face toward his until our lips met. The spark I'd felt at his touch on Thursday was now a simmering fire, flames that I must leave unattended as they cool to embers. Nevertheless, the longer we stood with our kiss deepening, the opposite was happening. An inferno was building.

"Listen to me," Patrick said when we finally pulled away. "Cash out. I saw the ledger. You have two million. That's twice the jackpot. Cash out and then," he reached into his pocket and produced a keycard, "go to the Hilton. I have the executive suite booked in your name. Leave this tournament now. I wish I could say more. I can only say that it's dangerous here."

I held the card in my hand as I contemplated his instructions.

"Danger," I said, looking back up, "is subjective, I've learned. Sometimes the safest place is in the middle of the fire."

His head shook. "I have to win the tournament, Maddie. I have to. I would never throw a game, but I would for you."

I took a step back. "Again, thank you for the vote of confidence. I wouldn't ask you or anyone else to throw the tournament. I will win. I'm fucking good."

"You're more than good," he said. "This...what's happening is big. There's more at stake than poker."

"I know that, Patrick. I'm well aware of the danger—as you put it—of not winning."

"Why didn't Leonardo bring you today?" he asked.

"What?" I was puzzled by his change in subject. "Why would you ask that?"

"I'm curious."

"I don't believe it is a big deal. He was called out of town. Marion came to my rescue. That was why I was late."

"Where did you find him? How did you hire him?"

My head shook, as if I could say *I have no say in my drivers or anyone else. They're all chosen for me.* Instead I answered, "Driver dot com. What difference does it make?"

"I have reason to believe Leonardo is connected to some

dangerous people, people who could be planning...things you don't need to know."

I did know that Mitchell was connected to dangerous people. I lived with the most dangerous one. However, whatever he was or wasn't planning wouldn't be discussed with me. I was certain he'd say it wasn't my concern. My concern was winning.

How would Patrick know anything about Mitchell's connection?

I handed the keycard back to Patrick. "What I know is that we need to get to the tournament. It's about time to begin play."

He reached for my hands, pushing the card back my way. "Take the keycard and the two million, and I will get you more, whatever you need. I want to win the tournament knowing you're safe."

"Then watch me win. At this moment, it's my best road to safety."

In the dimness, I watched as his eyes closed and opened. It was resignation. I wouldn't budge on my stance. I couldn't. He needed to accept that.

"May I kiss you once more?" he asked.

My hands went to his shoulders as I lifted my chin, bringing our lips close. Beneath my touch he seemed broader and harder. "Our goodbye kiss, Patrick."

Our lips met, fanning the flames of desire. I could try to ignore them, refuse to give them more fuel, yet that was impossible. The blaze was out of control. I'd heard once that wildfires had their usefulness, clearing away the undergrowth and giving birth to new life. The heat of the fire opened the outer coating of some pine cones, like popcorn, freeing the seeds to grow again.

In Patrick's arms, I would find that strength to remember the fire he tended within me and allow it to keep me warm in the future.

PATRICK

"He's here," Mason said as I approached the tournament hall.

I looked around, wondering if Madeline was already in the hall. I'd given her a few minutes' head start. "Who is?"

"Andros Ivanov."

Here?

Fuck.

"Reid was able to identify him through facial recognition," Mason went on. "He's in the tournament hall in the spectator section.

"Fuck," I said aloud, running my hand over the top of my head. "We need him surrounded."

"He is. Not only are you and I in there, we have Sparrows, ones we know we can trust."

"Do you think Ivanov has been trying to infiltrate our men?"

"I don't, but I'm not taking any chances where Sparrow is concerned."

"Would Ivanov try something here, tonight, during the tournament?" I asked.

"Sparrow doesn't think so. He said Ivanov knows he's outnumbered. Tonight he's a fucking peacock, strutting around, making himself known. A stranger can't take over a city. He needs to be seen and recognized. He needs to recruit and learn our weaknesses. Sparrow is sure that's what he's doing. Tomorrow we're beginning a shakedown on our men. We'll find out if anyone is disloyal."

I nodded, hoping the boss was right and tomorrow wasn't too late. "Tell me that Sparrow is still in Beckman's office."

"No." Mason nodded toward the hall where play was about to begin.

"Fuck."

"Listen, he's safe. He said he can't hide if Ivanov is making an appearance. This is his city and for the people who are here tonight, they need to know that."

"Play is about to begin," a woman said to those of us remaining in the hallway. "Once the doors are closed, they won't be reopened until the tournament is complete."

The woman speaking was wearing a black dress, reminding me of Ms. Standish. "Any new news from the police on Standish?"

"No. They haven't returned and Beckman has been radio silent like we told him to be."

"Is he still in the office wing?"

"Yes. Not a peep in hours. I should check on him, but I wanted to stay close to Sparrow," Mason replied.

"How many trusted Sparrows are here?"

"Ten inside the hall, with another twenty divided inside and outside of the club."

I nodded. "Let's get this tournament over. I'll feel better when all this hoopla quiets down and we can deal with regular shit."

"Regular shit sounds nice." Mason patted my shoulder. "You've got this."

A few minutes later, I was standing among the other remaining players awaiting our chair draw. Seating could seem insignificant to those less familiar with the game, but it was vitally important. The player dealt first in each hand rotated, from right to left of the dealer and play always progressed in the same fashion. If the person dealt before me drew three cards instead of two, I would then be subject to their decision, not receiving the card they drew.

I scanned the crowd. Andros Ivanov wasn't difficult to find. His love of the spotlight meant I'd seen his picture many times. He looked the same in person, dark hair and dark eyes. His Russian heritage showed in his features and his physical presence could be called intimidating. The Ivanov bratva earned their dominance like the rest of us—through force. He was surrounded by two big goons, neither of them Leonardo. They could have rented a neon sign and been as subtle.

"Number one," the announcer said. "Mr. Hillman."

The room filled with murmurs and applause as the tension built and Hillman took his seat in the first chair.

"Number two, Mr. Dunn."

The numbers continued as we began taking our seats.

"Number three, Mr. Kelly."

My gaze met Sparrow's. He was seated in a place of

importance where he could watch the room and no one but Sparrows could be behind him. Mason was on one side and Garrett on the other. With a somber expression, Sparrow nodded my way.

"Number four, Ms. Miller."

I sucked in a breath. While I was happy to sit with Maddie to my side, as she walked toward us in that fucking green dress, I had to remind myself to stay focused.

"Number five, Mr. Garcia."

"That would make me number six," Elliott said as the two men took the remaining two chairs.

"Our dealer tonight is..."

The room quieted as our stacks of chips were delivered. It appeared as it had on the ledger Sparrow had shown me. Elliott had the most. I was next and so on until Garcia, who appeared to have half of what Elliott did.

The dealer opened a new deck of cards, removing the seal and placing the cards into the shuffler. The dealer next removed the cards and offered them to Madeline. "Ms. Miller, would you like to cut the deck?"

She smiled. "No. I'm superstitious."

The room filled with nervous laughter. It was common among the elite poker players to not want to cut the deck, something about touching the cards before play. The dealer cut the deck and reinserted the cards to be shuffled.

I didn't believe in superstition and I doubted Maddie did either; nevertheless, it added to her persona.

"Shall we play?" the dealer asked.

And we did.

Betting remained high. The total number of chips remained

the same. It was their distribution that changed. It didn't take long before both Dunn and Garcia were out of money. The bets had exceeded their stacks.

Four of us remained.

An hour passed.

Another.

A closing time for tonight's play hadn't been set. We would play until a winner was crowned.

The cards fell where they did, making the play relatively even. With each passing hand, the crowd grew tenser. My gaze met Sparrow's. Without a word he told me to wrap this up.

The next hand was about to be dealt.

We all threw in our $5000 ante.

With Dunn eliminated, Hillman was on my left in the number one spot. However, the dealing had rotated, and in this hand, Madeline was dealt first, making me last with Elliott and Hillman in between.

One card.

Another.

Another.

Another.

Another.

They were all facedown and held close to our vests. This five-card stud was less entertaining to the crowd than Texas hold 'em.

We each examined our cards. As I did, I watched each player. Elliott and Madeline were deathly still, not giving away the slightest tell. It was Hillman who was unnecessarily boisterous. Experience told me that his behavior was too unpredictable. It could mean he had the cards or he didn't. It made his excessive tell as unenlightening as Elliott's and Madeline's lack thereof.

I fanned my cards: 5, 8, 9, 6, A.

It wasn't promising. The only thing going for me was that all the cards, with the exception of the ace, were diamonds. If I threw away the ace and drew another diamond, I would have a flush. The seven of diamonds would give me a straight flush. The flush had better odds. After all, there were thirteen cards of each suit in the deck. There was only one seven of diamonds. A flush could also be beaten by a royal flush, a straight flush, four of a kind, and a full house, in that order.

The bet began with Madeline.

"Fifty," she said.

Fifty thousand was a steep bet for before the draw.

Elliott peered her way. "I call your fifty." He reached for more chips. "And I raise you fifty."

The $100,000 bet was to Hillman. "Well, I probably shouldn't, but what the hell?" He pushed the adequate number of chips forward.

It was to me.

If when I drew, I drew neither a diamond nor a seven of diamonds I was left with the possibility of a nine high. Yet the possibility of more was there. I wouldn't fold. "I'll call," I said.

Madeline was the first to draw. "I'll take one," she said with her green eyes sparkling as she relinquished one card.

The card she was dealt was laid facedown before her, yet she didn't reach for it.

Interesting.

"One," Elliott said, laying one card from his hand down and receiving another.

"One," Hillman said, doing the same. He lifted his new card immediately. "Well, fuck me."

It was my turn.

I could keep the ace as a kicker and guarantee at least an ace high. I'd won with that in the past. They called it gambling for a reason. However, with everyone else drawing only one card, I didn't believe it would win this hand. I pulled the ace from my hand and laid it facedown on the table. "One."

The crowd murmured.

It was unusual for all the players to draw only one card.

Madeline lifted her new card. Her pleasure wasn't obvious, but I knew this woman. I felt the excitement radiating off of her, reverberating in waves. Whatever she had, she was pleased, very pleased.

I lifted my card and tucked it into my others without looking.

"Mr. Elliott," the dealer said. "You were the last to raise. The bet is to you."

Elliott eyed his stacks of chips. "I think it's time to make a move." He pushed one stack of $10,000 chips forward. And then he pushed another and another until his bet was one million.

The crowd hummed with excitement.

"Mr. Hillman, that's a million to you," the dealer said.

Hillman hemmed and hawed as he did inventory. He had the million to bet. We all did. Without his usual fanfare, he pushed a million dollars in chips forward.

"Mr. Kelly," the dealer said. "A million to you."

I slowly fanned my cards. 5, 6, 8, 9, and 7 of diamonds. I fought not to inhale as a straight flush, nine high, stared back at me. The only hand that could beat me was a higher straight flush, including a royal flush. I reached for my chips. "I see the million and raise another million."

The room around us erupted as club officials tried to shush the crowd.

"Ms. Miller," the dealer said. "That makes the bet two million to you."

Two million was what I'd told her to take, to leave with.

If only she would have.

"I see the two million, and I..." She pushed her all her stacks forward.

As she did, my heart dropped. Oh, my dear Maddie, don't do it.

"...I go all in."

This time it took longer for the room to still.

The bets went around the table. With a shit-eating grin, Elliott followed suit, pushing all his chips into the center. Hillman was next. We waited until finally, he did the same. It was my turn. I could fold and be the only remaining player against whoever won. That person would have the bulk of the money and a distinct advantage. My gaze met Sparrow's.

He was telling me to end this.

I pushed my chips to the center. This was it. "I'm in."

"Ms. Miller, everyone called," the dealer said, prompting her to reveal her hand.

Madeline nodded as she showed her cards: K, K, K, K, 10

"Ms. Miller has four of a kind, kings, and a ten."

The crowd gasped.

"Mr. Elliott," the dealer said.

Elliott tossed his hand to the table. "Well, doggie." The cards appeared: a straight: 10, 9, 8, 7, 6. Both black and red suits were represented. He smiled to Madeline. "I wish you the win."

"Thank you."

It was Hillman's turn. He turned his hand, one card at a time.

A.

A.

A.

The room gasped as Madeline's eyes grew wide. Four aces would beat her four kings. The thing was, I'd thrown an ace away, so I knew Hillman didn't have her beat. I wanted to reach out and reassure her. Even if I could, it would be hypocritical and short-lived.

Hillman flipped the last two at the same time: 8, 8.

"Aces high, full house," the dealer said.

Everyone turned to me.

With everything in me, I wanted to fold, to allow Maddie this win.

Could I choose Maddie over Sparrow?

I believed I could, but not where money and Chicago were at stake. For Madeline this was a game; she said she played for her survival. If it was money she needed, I'd give it to her. Hell, I'd play her in poker for it if she wouldn't accept the gift. I had no doubt that under other circumstances, Madeline Kelly was capable of kicking my ass at cards.

"Mr. Kelly."

I didn't draw it out. Instead, I turned my entire hand. 9, 8, 7, 6, and 5, all of diamonds.

"A straight flush."

Chairs moved as the room erupted.

"Ladies and gentlemen," Sparrow said loudly as he stood. "We will maintain order."

I reached over to Madeline, but she was also standing. Her expression of elation was gone, replaced by what could only be construed as fear.

"I can help you."

She straightened her neck. "No one can."

I sat dumbfounded as she made her way through the crowd to Ivanov.

Why would she go to him?

There was no question by the Detroit kingpin's expression, he was upset. With the volume and commotion of the room, I strained to hear what they were saying. The uproar won. That was all right, I didn't need to hear his words. Ivanov's body language alone had the small hairs on my neck standing on end.

The dealer was collecting the chips.

Sparrow and Mason came my way. "Good job," Sparrow said. "Let's go downstairs and get this figured out."

"What about..." I looked over to Andros Ivanov still talking to Maddie.

"We have Sparrows here," Mason said, looking at Sparrow. "Both Ivanov and Hillman and their respective crew will be escorted off the property as soon as we are secure."

Our number-one job was keeping the boss, Sterling Sparrow, safe.

I looked from my friends to Maddie and back again. "I will explain this soon—I've tried already—but first I have to be sure of something. My gut is telling me something isn't right." I looked at Mason and tipped my chin toward Sparrow. "Get him downstairs."

The commotion grew louder around Ivanov and his men with Maddie right in the middle.

Sometimes it's safest in the middle of the fire.

Oh hell no. I couldn't stand by any longer.

Ivanov's voice came into range. "I told you what would happen if you lost."

"Get the other spectators out of here," I ordered, speaking to a Sparrow capo. "I want this hall cleared."

"No, no, you didn't say that," Maddie's voice cracked. "Andros, I'm sorry. I had a great hand. You saw it. It was dealt to me. I was so sure." With each sentence her desperation mushroomed, causing the words to come faster and faster.

I walked closer, leaving Mason and Sparrow with other Sparrows.

"Please...don't do this," she said, holding onto his arm.

He reached for her hand and roughly pushed it away.

I moved closer. "Don't touch the lady."

Ivanov's laughter resonated above the crowd noise. It wasn't only his. Now Hillman and his men were circling the others.

"Lady?" Ivanov asked. "You have the wrong woman." He eyed Madeline. "This one's a loser."

My fist came forward. Before I had time to think, it collided with his arrogant jaw.

"No," Madeline screamed as her hands came to her lips.

Ivanov staggered backward as his arms went out. "Wait," he demanded, holding back his men as they lurched forward, their eyes on me. "No, not yet." He regained his position as he rubbed his chin.

"Get out of my club—now. Your invitation has expired."

I knew the deep, commanding voice. It was Sparrow.

Fuck. He needed to get out of here.

"Your club? You think this club is yours?" Ivanov asked. "You probably think the city is yours too. You're wrong. I have parts, and soon I will have it all."

"Get the fuck out now," Sparrow said, his words demanding yet his tone eerily calm, "and you will live to see tomorrow."

"Come," Ivanov said to the men gathered. "We'll be back." He nodded to Mason. "Better check on the man in the office. He was no longer useful to me."

What?

Mason's gaze met mine.

Was he talking about Beckman?

By the time I turned to Madeline, she was walking, her head down, following Ivanov's and Hillman's men as they exited the room.

"Madeline, stay here," I said, ignoring the way Sparrow and Mason were looking at me.

Her head shook. "I can't, Patrick."

"Man," Mason said, reaching for my shoulder, "whatever is happening, let her go."

Ivanov stopped and turned to Madeline. "I told you that returning required a win." His gaze came to me. "Keep her. Her usefulness is also done. I have the newer version." His lips curled into a smile. "She's something else...fresh, innocent, and even more beautiful."

"No, Andros. I'll do anything," Madeline called out as Ivanov and his men continued to leave.

"Make sure they are escorted off the property," Sparrow was saying.

"Please, you promised," she pleaded, her voice growing louder.

"And you promised me a win." Those were his last words.

My attention went to Madeline as I tried to make sense of what happened, what was happening. In the few minutes since the last game she had crumpled. I went to her as she leaned forward sobbing as if she'd been hit in the stomach.

Standing taller, she looked up at me with tear-filled eyes. "I told you I had to win." She looked at me, Mason, and Sparrow. "Please, if you can, stop him. I have to go with him."

"Maddie, you don't understand who he is," I said.

She nodded. "I do. I know exactly who he is."

"Patrick, what—?" Sparrow began.

"I've been trying to tell you—"

Madeline's gut-wrenching wail stopped my reply.

I reached for her arm. "I'm going to tell them."

"I-it doesn't matter," she muttered, sobs hiccupping her words. Mascara and tears covered her cheeks as blotches filled her neck and chest. "Y-you don't understand."

I reached again for Madeline's arms, no longer caring about Sparrow and Mason. "I *understand* you're my wife. I'll keep you safe."

"Patrick," she said, trying to catch her breath. "I have to go with Andros."

"You don't have to."

"I do. He has my—" Her glassy green eyes stared up at me. "Patrick, Andros has *our* daughter."

Thank you for reading *SPARK*.
Patrick and Madeline's story continues in *FLAME* and concludes in *ASHES*. You're not going to want to miss a moment of *WEB OF DESIRE*. Both *Flame* and *Ashes* are now available for pre-order.

And if you haven't read *WEB OF SIN*, Sterling Sparrow and Araneae's story, begin the **completed trilogy** today reading *SECRETS*, book 1 of Web of Sin.

Lastly, if you haven't read *TANGLED WEB*, Mason/Kader and Laurel's story, begin the **completed trilogy** today by reading *TWISTED*, book #1 Tangled Web.

WHAT TO DO NOW

LEND IT: Did you enjoy SPARK? Do you have a friend who'd enjoy SPARK? SPARK may be lent one time. Sharing is caring!

RECOMMEND IT: Do you have multiple friends who'd enjoy my dark romance with twists and turns and an all new sexy and infuriating anti-hero? Tell them about it! Call, text, post, tweet...your recommendation is the nicest gift you can give to an author!

REVIEW IT: Tell the world. Please go to the retailer where you purchased this book, as well as Goodreads, and write a review. Please share your thoughts about SPARK on:

*Amazon, SPARK Customer Reviews

*Barnes & Noble, SPARK, Customer Reviews

*Apple Books, SPARK Customer Reviews

* BookBub, SPARK Customer Reviews

*Goodreads.com/Aleatha Romig

BOOKS BY NEW YORK TIMES BESTSELLING AUTHOR ALEATHA ROMIG

THE SPARROW WEBS:

WEB OF DESIRE:

SPARK

Releasing January 14, 2020

FLAME

Releasing February 25, 2020

ASHES

Releasing April 7, 2020

TANGLED WEB:

TWISTED

Released May, 2019

OBSESSED

Released July, 2019

BOUND

Released August, 2019

WEB OF SIN:

SECRETS

Released October, 2018

LIES

Released December, 2018

PROMISES

Released January, 2019

THE INFIDELITY SERIES:

BETRAYAL

Book #1

Released October 2015

CUNNING

Book #2

Released January 2016

DECEPTION

Book #3

Released May 2016

ENTRAPMENT

Book #4

Released September 2016

FIDELITY

Book #5

Released January 2017

THE CONSEQUENCES SERIES:

CONSEQUENCES

(Book #1)

Released August 2011

TRUTH

(Book #2)

Released October 2012

CONVICTED

(Book #3)

Released October 2013

REVEALED

(Book #4)

Previously titled: Behind His Eyes Convicted: The Missing Years

Re-released June 2014

BEYOND THE CONSEQUENCES

(Book #5)

Released January 2015

RIPPLES

Released October 2017

CONSEQUENCES COMPANION READS:

BEHIND HIS EYES-CONSEQUENCES

Released January 2014

BEHIND HIS EYES-TRUTH

Released March 2014

STAND ALONE MAFIA THRILLER:

PRICE OF HONOR

Available Now

THE LIGHT DUET:

Published through Thomas and Mercer Amazon exclusive

INTO THE LIGHT

Released June, 2016

AWAY FROM THE DARK

Released October, 2016

TALES FROM THE DARK SIDE SERIES:

INSIDIOUS

(All books in this series are stand-alone erotic thrillers)

Released October 2014

ALEATHA'S LIGHTER ONES:

PLUS ONE

Stand-alone fun, sexy romance

Released May 2017

A SECRET ONE

Fun, sexy novella

Released April 2018

ANOTHER ONE

Stand-alone fun, sexy romance

Releasing May 2018

ONE NIGHT

Stand-alone, sexy contemporary romance

September 2017

INDULGENCE SERIES:

UNEXPECTED

Released August, 2018

UNCONVENTIONAL

Released January, 2018

UNFORGETTABLE

Released October, 2019

ABOUT THE AUTHOR

Aleatha Romig is a New York Times, Wall Street Journal, and USA Today bestselling author who lives in Indiana, USA. She has raised three children with her high school sweetheart and husband of over thirty years. Before she became a full-time author, she worked days as a dental hygienist and spent her nights writing. Now, when she's not imagining mind-blowing twists and turns, she likes to spend her time with her family and friends. Her other pastimes include reading and creating heroes/anti-heroes who haunt your dreams!

Aleatha impresses with her versatility in writing. She released her first novel, CONSEQUENCES, in August of 2011. CONSEQUENCES, a dark romance, became a bestselling series with five novels and two companions released from 2011 through 2015. The compelling and epic story of Anthony and Claire Rawlings has graced more than half a million e-readers. Her first stand-alone smart, sexy thriller INSIDIOUS was next. Then Aleatha released the five-novel INFIDELITY series, a romantic suspense saga, that took the reading world by storm, the final book landing on three of the top bestseller lists. She ventured into traditional publishing with Thomas and Mercer. Her books INTO THE LIGHT and AWAY FROM THE DARK were published through this mystery/thriller publisher in 2016. In the spring of 2017, Aleatha again ventured into a different genre with her first fun and sexy stand-alone romantic comedy with the USA Today bestseller PLUS ONE. She continued with ONE NIGHT and ANOTHER ONE. If you like fun, sexy, novellas that make your heart pound, try her UNCONVENTIONAL and UNEXPECTED. In 2018 Aleatha returned to her dark romance roots with WEB OF SIN.

Aleatha is a "Published Author's Network" member of the Romance Writers of America, NINC, and PEN America. She is represented by Kevan Lyon of Marsal Lyon Literary Agency.

f facebook.com/aleatharomig

twitter.com/aleatharomig

instagram.com/aleatharomig

CPSIA information can be obtained
at www.ICGtesting.com
Printed in the USA
LVHW031942090120
643080LV00007B/1069/P